Tanzil's Second Chance

A Bear's Cove Novel

by

A·J· Stone

Bear's Cove 2: Tanzil's Second Chance
Copyright © April 2018 by A.J. Stone
Print ISBN: 978-1-942414-56-8

Editor: Nicoline Tiernan
Cover Artist: Anne Kay
Published by Lost Goddess Publishing LLC

A Warden's job is to protect

Six years ago, Tanzil Jareth failed to protect his family. To atone for that, he has dedicated his life to protecting all bear shifters from the humans who would exploit or kill them. When a hiking bear shifter goes missing, nothing was going to keep Tanzil from rescuing him.

Lost with nowhere to go

Logan Fordline doesn't know what he wants in life. Nothing he's tried has suited him. So he decides to spend a few days roaming in his bear form to try to figure out what he's supposed to do with his life. Of course, he didn't think that he'd be targeted by humans hoping to show him off as a freak attraction.

Rescuing Logan wasn't that difficult, but resisting the chemistry between them is impossible. Will Tanzil be able to put the past behind him and move forward with a new love, and will Logan find a path in life that leaves him fulfilled and happy?

Welcome to Bear's Cove, a hidden community of gay bear shifters. Tanzil's Second Chance is a 33,000-word, gay male pregnancy romance that includes passionate and explicit sexual content, including bondage, light D/s, and violence. Suitable for adult audiences.

Prologue—Logan

"How long are you going to be gone?"

Logan Fordline glanced up from securing his frame pack in the back of his pickup truck. His best friend, Chase Longfellow stood on the other side of the bed, his arms crossed and his bottom lip sticking out. Logan chuffed a laugh. "You won't miss me. Dak will keep you occupied, for sure."

A faint flush stole up Chase's cheeks, and he slapped a hand on the back of his neck. He and Chase had a lot in common, or at least, they used to. The blond pair used to tear up the town on the weekend—partying all night, raising hell, and hooking up with whatever hot alpha caught their interest.

Now Chase was married and pregnant with his first child.

So much had changed in a short time. Now when Logan looked at Chase, all he saw were the differences. Logan's blond hair was sandier, and he had blue eyes to Chase's soft brown ones. Chase had started an appliance repair business that was doing quite well, and Logan chafed under the restrictions of working in a law office.

Chase was finished with the juvenile phase of his life, and he'd made some changes, including setting new parameters for their friendship. No longer would he allow Logan to take him for granted.

Dak's influence had wrought these changes in his best friend, and it had made Logan realize a few things. Namely, he'd been a shitty friend to Chase, and Chase had stuck with him far longer than he deserved. Also law school had not been his idea. He'd gone along with it to please his fathers, and that was the wrong reason to choose a path in life.

In short, Logan was not happy with his life, and he wasn't sure how to change it. One thing was for certain—staying in the same place and doing the same thing wasn't going to make anything happen for him.

Finally, Chase stamped his foot. "Are you going to be back in time for the baby?"

"Yeah, of course. I'm going for a week, maybe two. I just need..." Logan shook his head, uncertain how to explain it. "I need to clear my head. Reconnecting with nature, spending time in bear form—that's what I need right now."

Chase came around the back of the truck and, due to his protruding belly, maneuvered in for a sideways hug. "Be safe. I'm going to miss you."

Though he was tempted to make a remark about how Dak wouldn't leave Chase enough time to miss Logan, he swallowed it down and accepted the sweetness of the sentiment. "I'll miss you too, buddy."

He opened the passenger side of his truck and took out a small gift bag, which he gave to Chase.

Chase eyed it curiously. "For me?"

"Sort of. It's for the baby."

Chase's lower jaw dropped open. "My first baby gift! Can I open it?"

"That's why I'm giving it to you now."

Without waiting a second longer, Chase dug into the bag. He held the gift up between them, his curious gaze going between the brown onesie with a hood that made it look like a bear's ears. It had hand and foot flaps he'd made to resemble bear paws, and the tail was part of the pattern on the back. Logan didn't think anyone would enjoy laying on an actual tail, and he figured it was also a choking or strangulation hazard.

It didn't take Chase long to assemble the puzzle pieces. "You made this?"

Logan shrugged. "You said it would be cute, but I couldn't find anything in the stores. So I got a pattern, and Simone let me use her sewing machine." He didn't add that he'd watched hundreds of hours of sewing videos online, and Simone had helped him with some style issues during his first few runs at making the garment. He was proud of the final product.

A sheen of tears wet Chase's eyes. "It's really good. I mean, you've always loved fashion, but this is really, really good."

A thunk sounded from the other side of the truck. Logan peered over Chase's shoulder to see Dak securing a bag. Dak was a large alpha, broad-shouldered and thickly muscled. His short dark hair grazed his forehead, and his blue eyes smiled at Logan and Chase. He'd recently transferred his sheriff's job back to Bear's Cove because that's where Chase wanted to live.

"What's that?" Logan wasn't sure he wanted to carry more than what could fit on his frame pack. When he shifted, he'd have to stow those things anyway.

"Waterproof matches, bug spray, an axe, and a couple of citronella candles."

2

Logan wrinkled his nose. "I'm going to be in bear form. I won't need all that."

A husky laugh fell from Dak, who hailed from an outlying area like the one Logan planned to visit. "You'll thank me later."

He came around the truck and hugged both Chase and Logan. Then the trio separated.

"Now, when you get out there, be careful not to wander out of the protected areas. Bears are wanderers at heart, and that sometimes makes it hard to gauge how far out you really are. But if you open your senses, you should have no problem sensing the Wards." Dak drummed his fingers on the edge of the bed and looked toward the sky as he thought. "What else? Oh, avoid interacting with humans. It's bear-hunting season, and humans are assholes most of the time." He shot Chase an apologetic look as he added that addendum. Chase's mother had been human.

Wards were magical spells that kept humans from taking too much notice of the shifter settlements dotting the New England coast. Most humans reacted badly when confronted with the idea of shifters in general, kidnapping them for study or display, or just killing them out of fear or spite.

Chase chewed his lip, and Logan knew his friend was thinking about his mother, and how her own father had killed her rather than let her live as the wife of a bear shifter.

Dak, always sensitive to Chase's emotions, slid an arm around his husband's shoulders and pulled him closer.

"Just be careful," Chase said. He rubbed a hand over his swollen abdomen. "And come back before the baby comes. I know fuck-all about raising kids."

Neither did Logan. He climbed into the cab of his truck and grinned at his friends. "I know you shouldn't swear around them. Maybe start curbing that habit right now?"

With a mighty roar of laughter, Dak said, "We're working on that, Logan. Don't you worry."

Judging from the crimson staining his fair-skinned friend's face, Logan figured a spanking was on the horizon for Chase, but it probably wouldn't be a deterrent. Chase loved a good spanking.

Logan swallowed down a twinge of jealousy. He didn't want Chase or Dak, but he wouldn't mind someone who looked at him the way Dak looked at Chase. That would be nice.

Chapter 1—Logan

The frame pack, food, and tent were part of the back-up plan. Logan planned to rough it in the purest sense of the word. Because he'd never done that before, he'd let Chase and Dak talk him into taking along provisions. Well, mostly Dak had campaigned for that action. As a deputy for Bear's Cove and a former resident of Forrest Hills, Dak had more experience spending time in bear form and in the woods.

Logan was a city boy, born and raised. While he'd gone for weekend camping trips, his fathers had been along to take care of him, and they'd taken a camper. Roughing it meant cooking on a tiny stove and sleeping on a lumpy mattress that doubled as a sofa during the day.

This time, Logan wanted to leave all that behind. He parked his truck in a small dirt lot surrounded by trees. In the narrow strip of brown grass along the margin were three picnic tables and green metal trash cans. Though the weather was cooler, it was a fine fall day, and only one other vehicle was around.

He leaned on the side of his truck, closed his eyes, and set free his ursine senses. Scents not found in the city assailed his nose—the faint odor of other animals, fallen leaves rotting on the ground, and the crispness of the air. The alarm that had been blaring inside his mind for the past few months finally settled down to a dull, faraway beep that barely registered.

This was exactly what he needed.

"Hey, there. Heading out?"

Opening his eyes, he looked toward the sound of the voice, and his heart skipped a beat. Standing there was the most handsome man Logan had ever seen. Though he was a few inches taller than Logan, this man had impossibly broad shoulders. His dark hair reflected the sun, shining like silk, and Logan's fingers itched to find out if it really was that soft. The man's skin was darker, like cinnamon and honey, and just the idea of tasting it made Logan's mouth water.

Mostly his eyes captured Logan's interest. The man had deep brown eyes, bottomless pools that he could enjoy drowning in.

With a start, Logan gave himself a mental shake and wiped the flirty smile off his face. He wasn't here to hook up. He was here to figure out why his life wasn't working for him and what kinds of changes would take it in a direction that would fulfill him.

"Hi."

The man's gaze held Logan's, even though Logan wanted nothing more than to look away. "Planning on a day trip or something longer?"

Logan frowned. These were not questions a stranger asked, not unless they had nefarious intentions. "What's it to you?"

Tall, Dark, and Handsome indicated his badge. "Conservation officer Tanzil Jareth. U.S. Fish and Wildlife Service."

"Oh." Heat traveled up Logan's neck. The guy wore a brown uniform and drove a truck with the emblem emblazoned on the side. "Sorry. I didn't realize. My name is Logan Fordline. I'm planning to do some hiking for a couple of weeks."

The officer peeked into the bed of Logan's truck. "A couple of weeks? You're alone, and that's a long time."

Logan shrugged. "I need some time to get in touch with my wild side."

The man nodded sagely. "All young bears should do that. Be careful. I'll check back in a few days." With that, he got in his truck and left the small lot.

Logan glanced around, searching for a place to hide his keys. The only negative thing about shifting was the lack of pockets. Overhead on a branch seemed like the best option.

He undressed, threw his clothes into the cab of his truck, and put his keys in a waterproof pouch. Then he climbed onto the hood, stretched his 5'10 frame as high as it could reach, and secured the pouch to a limb. From the ground, it was invisible. As long as no enterprising raccoon found it, he'd be fine.

Then he shifted into his bear form and took off. There was a trail a few feet away, but that was for hikers, and he had no wish to run into anyone while he was out and about. Huffing and chuffing, he explored the forest.

Time passed differently for a bear. No thoughts invaded his mind, nagging him to figure out why he felt like someone else was living his life while he watched from the sidelines.

He roamed, nibbling on nuts and roots as he tasted his way deeper into the woods. With each step, his life as a human seemed farther away and less meaningful. Tension in his shoulders, stress from too much uncertainty, melted away. He barely noticed when night fell.

Eventually he found himself on the edge of a small, rocky clearing. Moss and hardscrabble trees clung to crevices. Further on, the rocks grew larger as they melded with the mountainside. Logan toyed with the notion of climbing it, but then he tossed away the idea. The open area provided no cover, and he spied no worthwhile food in that

5

direction. Off to the north, a waterfall marked the head of a stream—and that meant fish.

Fish sounded great right now. His mouth salivated just thinking about it.

He turned around, intent on forging a path to water, and the world went dark.

Shooting pain seared through his head, hitting the point behind his eye that made him groan. Logan lifted a hand and pressed it to his temple. He squeezed his eyes shut tightly, fighting the inevitable. In all the times he'd passed out drunk, this was by far the worst. His entire body seemed to throb in time to the pain in his head, and he'd never been so fucking cold in his life.

Reluctantly, Logan peeled open an eyelid. Light streamed through metal bars, and his breath fogged where it left his mouth. The sun, a tiny orange ball in the sky, was mostly obscured by the tall trees surrounding him.

He sat up, noting he was naked and in human form. Memories slowly penetrated the miasma that had turned his brain to mush. He'd been in ursine form, roaming free. Had something hit him?

He checked his body for damage and found welts in his shoulder and thigh. "Somebody fucking tasered me?"

Bars surrounded him, and he realized he was in a cage.

That shock crispened the thoughts in his head. He looked around, taking stock of his situation. Behind him, he found a small cabin with a huge pile of firewood stacked against a wall under an overhang. Smoke rose from the chimney.

Logan thought about calling out, but a warning bell clanging in his head clashed with the headache to silence him. Someone had put him in a cage. And he was naked.

It was likely he'd been in bear form when they'd tasered him.

He inspected the cage, looking for a latch. A bear might not be able to open a sliding bolt, but in his human form, he sure as hell could. Why the fuck would someone taser a bear and stick him in cage anyway?

But the cage had a padlock, the kind that needed a key.

Fuck. What the hell had happened?

The door in the rear of the house opened, and instinct had him shifting back into bear form. Instantly he was warmer. He watched, wary and afraid, as a woman emerged. She had long blonde hair tied up in a ponytail. It flowed halfway down her back. In deference to the cold, she wore boots, and her long jacket covered most of her body.

As she approached, he smelled raw fish, and he noted the metal bowl she carried. He sat back on his haunches, ready to spring at her if she opened the cage door.

She stopped a few feet away, out of reach of his paw should he lean through the bars to swipe at her.

He sounded a warning growl, a deep noise rumbling from this throat.

Her eyes widened, but her mouth curved up in a placating smile. "It's okay, boy. I won't hurt you."

Logan was already hurt. Now he wanted out of the cage. He didn't react to her vocalization.

"My name is Emily." She glanced around, a brief frown wrinkling her chin. "Be right back."

He watched as she retreated to a small wooden shed ten feet away and disappeared inside.

When she returned, she had a broom, the kind with the wide head meant for sweeping large areas. She set the bowl on the grass and used the horizontal wooden piece that held the bristles to slide it across the uneven ground. "I thought you'd be hungry by now."

Logan was starving. A bear his size could easily eat fifty pounds in one sitting. Whatever was in that bowl wouldn't be enough. As it neared him, he noted the fruit and nuts mixed in with the raw salmon in the feed bowl. It clanked against the bars of the cage, too wide to fit through the small gap.

"Oh." Her face fell. "I didn't think that through too well, did I?"

The bear part of his nature wanted the food even though he was wary. Logan rose to stand on his hind legs, wrapped his front paws around the bars, and shook the cage with all his might. The whole kennel was perhaps five feet square and four feet tall. The floor and ceiling were made of mesh. Logan noted the weak points, and he shook harder, aiming to knock the contraption on its side.

He expected Emily to lift the broom and whack his paws—at the very least she should back away—but she only pressed her lips together. "Come now, you cute little bear shifter, you know better than to behave that way. You're going to hurt yourself."

At this point, Logan didn't care if he hurt himself. He didn't know how long he'd been unconscious and in his human form. He'd spent, at the very least, several hours caged and exposed to the elements. He shook harder, but the structure held fast.

"It's anchored into the ground with steel poles and cement. That cage isn't going to budge. Eat your breakfast." Without waiting for him to respond, she went back into the cabin.

Logan prowled the cage, pushing and swatting at the bars as he inspected the construction. Everything had a weak point. In the meantime, his stomach growled. Giving into temptation, he stuck his face through the bars and ate the scant offering. After a while, exhaustion overtook him. He curled up in the center of the cage, his eyes too heavy to fight even though he knew he needed to stay awake.

"Fucking bitch drugged me," he growled as sleep stole his consciousness.

The next time he woke, Emily stood outside the cage. She grinned when she saw his eyes were open. "I hope you had a good nap. What are the chances you'll shift into your human form and talk with me?"

One sniff, and Logan knew Emily wasn't a shifter. He thought about his friend Chase, how Chase's parents had been murdered by humans, and he decided against shifting.

In his bear form, it was harder to think logically. He could act and react, forage or fight, but clear and rational thinking was better done in human form. So he went with his instincts and remained as he was.

She crouched down next to the bars. "I won't hurt you. I promise that it's okay. I just want to see what you look like as a man."

He watched through wary eyes as she spoke, her gentle tones pleading and encouraging, but he held fast to his plan. Later, when she brought dinner, he didn't partake.

When the sun set, he prowled the cage. Hungry, tired, and pissed off, he wouldn't think twice before tearing the head off anyone who came near him. Hours passed. The moon peeked through the trees, and Emily returned.

He'd only been in captivity for a day, and already he was happy to see his captor.

But this time she had a companion.

"He won't eat," she said. "I think he knows I put sedatives in his breakfast."

The man with her was taller than her, but shorter than Logan in his human form. Where Logan was lean and lithe, this guy was round. He had enough fat to survive a winter's hibernation. Logan did not. The man's beard hid a lot of his face, and his eyebrows were bushy enough

8

to support wildlife. He stroked the bottom bush as he thought, and then he shook his head. "No, Em. These creatures aren't that smart. He's a small one, and skinny. Maybe he's diseased?"

Emily's eyes flared. "He's fine. You leave him alone."

"Not much meat." The man shrugged. "I vote for making jerky sooner rather than later."

Bears were scavengers, omnivorous creatures who would eat anything, but shifters were a bit more discerning in their tastes. Logan vowed to never again eat jerky.

"Hey, there you are." A third person, another male, jogged around the side of the cabin, coming toward them. Though he greatly resembled the hairy man, this guy was taller and less rotund. "Has he shifted yet?"

Emily's gaze fell sharply before rising to look over Logan. "No. I texted you everything there was to know."

"Which is nothing." There was an edge to his statement, making it an accusation.

"Give me a break, Jared. I have things to do." Emily huffed, rolled her eyes, and said Jared's name as if spitting out rotten cauliflower.

"Yeah, sleeping and watching nature shows." Jared snorted. He didn't seem to notice her derision.

"I like to know what we're up against."

"Shows about bears ain't gonna teach you shit about bear shifters. This is a whole different species." Jared rolled his eyes and looked to the first man for support.

The first man rocked back on his heels. "Very little is known about bear shifters. They're as like to kill you as look at you. We should've electrified the cage."

"We'd need a bigger generator," Jared said. "Feed him again, Em. This time don't put anything in it."

Emily returned to the house.

The bearded man stepped closer. "Listen up, fucker. Emily has a soft spot for you because she likes animals, but Jared and me don't. You're gonna perform for us, or you're not gonna eat. Got it?"

Logan didn't move. One more step, he thought. Just a little closer.

"Don't get so close, Chad. He's liable to be rabid."

"Nah. He's not even moving. Looking at how small he is, I bet he's starving. We'll have to get him up a hundred pounds or so before we can show him off." Chad scooted closer and crouched down. "You're a cute little fella, ain't ya?"

The fucker was in reach. Logan lunged, his claws flashing moments before he sank them into Chad's shoulder.

9

Chad shrieked, the high-pitched noise music to Logan's ears.

Now that he had a grip, he jerked Chad closer, clanging his head into the bars of the cage. Electricity raced through his body, and not the good kind either. This kind shook his eyeballs and scrambled his brain. With a mighty bellow, he dropped Chad and swung at the thing stinging him.

Not a taser—this was a cattle prod. He dislodged the tip from his side, as another sting penetrated his flank, and the world swam out of focus.

Fuck, he thought. That did not go as planned.

When he woke this time, he wasn't as cold. The bare dirt below him had been warmed by his body heat, and now it was the warmest part of him. He glanced around, furtively looking to see if his captors had gone. The darkness of night had deepened, but in his bear form, his night vision was better than in his human form. He made out the same shapes he'd seen before—trees surrounding a cabin and a small shed. This was not what he'd envisioned when he'd packed up for a couple weeks of camping. Maybe he should have actually gone camping.

He lumbered to his feet, his body shaking with exhaustion and residual pain from taking so many volts of electricity. And was that a tranquilizer dart in his left hip? He partially morphed his paw into a hand to remove the offending item. Yes, that was a tranquilizer dart. Either Jared or Emily had done that, since he was certain he'd caused major damage to Chad's shoulder.

A light over the back entrance came on, and Emily hopped down the two wooden steps with a small bowl in her one hand and a flashlight in the other. She smiled as she came closer. "I see you're up. It's almost morning, sleepyhead. How about some breakfast? You skipped dinner."

Part of him wanted to lunge at her, but the rest of him was too hungry to attack. He backed up to show that he wasn't a threat.

She set the bowl down and got the broom to push it to where he could reach. The moment the broom made contact with the bowl, the screen door on the back slammed open.

"Emily, you crazy bitch, get away from that bear."

Emily froze at the name he used, and her lips pushed out in a pout. "I'm feeding him. He hasn't eaten much in two days, and he was already skinny when we found him. He's like to die."

Jared snatched up the bowl of nourishment. "You know who's like to die? Chad, that's who." He stalked back toward the cabin.

On his heels, Emily followed. "Don't you think Chad would want him in good shape? You can't show a shifter in bad shape. They don't shift."

The rest of their argument was lost as they went inside, though Logan had no problem hearing their voices raised in anger.

Three days passed before Emily appeared again, though Jared had come by a few times. He'd watch Logan, his brown eyes searching for something, probably a clue that Logan was, in fact, a shifter and not just a run-of-the-mill brown bear.

Too weak to lift his head, Logan peered through the bars of the cage.

Emily crept closer. She threw something into the cage and ran back to the cabin.

The item landed near Logan's mouth. Salmon. Raw. Whole. He forced himself to gulp it down, and then he closed his eyes. This dreamless sleep wasn't drug-induced, but the product of exhaustion.

The odor of strawberries a few days past their prime woke him next. He found a small mound of the mushy, red fruit inside the cage, and he gulped it down in two bites. The flavor was off, but a starving bear couldn't afford to have standards.

Emily's small gifts continued to keep him going, but it wasn't enough to rejuvenate him. He couldn't even tell how much time passed between meals.

He woke sometime later—days or hours—to find Emily petting him through the bars of the cage. "It's okay, boy. I'm doing the best I can, but Jared wants you dead, and Chad is still in the hospital. You did him real bad, and then he got some kind of hospital supervirus that kicked his ass."

Serves him right, Logan thought. Karma's a bitch, asshole with a cattle prod.

"If you behave, you'll get more food. All we want is to show you off, make a little money. People will pay big bucks to see a bear who can turn into a man." She stroked his head as if he were a pet dog.

He resisted the urge to bite her. Right now, she was the only person interested in feeding him.

"If you wanted to shift into human form, I could get you some clothes. I don't know how big you are, but I have some size XXL sweats I got from the charity box."

If he'd been in his right mind, Logan would have been offended. For most of his life, he'd spent time honing his body to physical perfection. He was handsome and built, two things Emily's companions were not.

She stayed, talking to him as she petted his head, for a long time. The injustice nagged at him, but the soothing physical touch and the human contact did a lot to assuage the loneliness and desperation that was a heavy stone in his gut.

Logan nodded off, and when he woke, Emily was gone.

She'd fed him enough so he had energy to lumber to his feet. As he'd dozed, an idea had come to him. The floor of the cage was dirt. He'd dig near one side and tunnel under the structure. The posts might be set into concrete, but there were only four of them, one at each corner.

He set to work. He waited for his claws to make significant progress, but the earth beneath him was hard-packed, and he was weak. After digging for what felt like hours, he looked down to find a hole almost six inches deep. This was not going well. He needed sustenance.

The light over the back porch came on again. Logan laid over the small dent in the ground. It would suck to lose even this small bit of progress.

The light shining behind the figure showed a silhouette he'd come to know as Jared's. The man meandered closer, his staggering steps betraying his drunken state. He stopped inches from the cage, fumbling with a flashlight.

"Fuckin' thing won't turn on." He wrestled with it a moment longer before tossing it to the ground. "Don't need a fuckin' light to do what I came to do. You killed Chad, you motherfucker. He's dead, an' now you're gonna be dead."

He lifted his hand. Thunder crackled through the air, and a searing pain lanced across Logan's side. A soulful cry of pain issued from his throat, a single sound that gave his captor power. Logan hated that he'd been so weak as much as he hated the fear roiling his insides. He was going to die here, alone and in a cage. He'd become just another bear who'd chosen to leave Bear's Cove and had never returned.

But unlike those bears, Logan didn't have a choice. Unlike those bears, Logan didn't want to live in bear form all the time. He liked being human. He liked walking and talking, having a beer with friends, and hooking up with anyone who struck his fancy.

"What are you doing?" Emily's high-pitched voice screeched through the night, sending small critters fleeing. "Are you crazy?"

"Chad's dying. I'm gonna kill this fuckin' bear. He's not a shifter."

"You don't know that." She set a hand on his shoulder. "Jared, Chad isn't dead. They're giving him medicine. It's going to take time."

Jared shook his head. "I ain't never seen him like this. He's dying. My baby brother is dying, and it's all this damn bear's fault." He lifted his hand with the gun in it.

Emily stepped in front of the gun. "Jared, don't. Chad is going to get better, and he's going to want this bear alive and well when he wakes up. You know what this means to him."

She said some things, but her voice was too quiet for Logan to hear above the throbbing pain growing to a roar in his ears.

Jared's body swayed. "It's not a shifter. All the other ones had shifted by now. Starve 'em a few days, and they turn into their humanlike form so they can sweet talk you."

"Just give it another day, okay? Chad will wake up, and we'll ask him what he wants to do." She pulled her robe tighter around her body. "Jared, be patient."

Without warning, Jared's hand shot out, and he slammed the butt of the handgun against Emily's head. Her body crumpled to the ground, and Jared followed it down, his fists flailing as he beat her body and yelled. He called her all sorts of names, but nothing he said seemed substantive. He was pissed and an abusive asshole, and she was the nearest target.

Finally Jared rolled away.

Emily's quiet sobs filled the silence.

Having been in his share of brawls, Logan felt for the woman—not a ton because she was responsible for keeping him in a cage—but he'd thought she'd been unconscious for the beating.

"You want to keep this bear alive, he's gonna have to eat." Jared pointed the gun at Logan as he unlatched the door to the cage.

Logan wanted to lunge for the opening, but he was too weak. Starvation and the loss of blood from having been shot had sapped all his energy.

Jared snatched Emily up by the hair and shoved her into the cage. The door slammed shut behind her. She stumbled a few steps, but then she whirled, flying to the door. "You can't lock me in here—especially not with a wounded bear. Chad will kill you when he finds out what you've done."

"Chad's dying, you stupid bitch, and you're going to die with him. This was your idea. I know Chad didn't think up this on his own. I know this was you. You killed my brother just as much as that fucking bear did, and you can both starve to death." With that, he stumbled back toward the house. Halfway there, he tripped and fell on his face. He didn't get up.

Emily growled. "Motherfucker passed out."

Then she must have realized she was in a cage with a hungry, wounded bear because she turned around and stared, wide-eyed, at Logan. Part of him wanted to hurt her. The scent of her blood mixed with his and permeated the small space. He wanted to finish the job Jared had begun, but a larger piece of him didn't want to be lumped in with that deplorable bastard.

He watched her shrink into the farthest corner of the cage and curl into a defensive ball.

Fuck. Now he wasn't going to be able to finish tunneling out.

Chapter 2—Tanzil

Being a game warden, or a conservation officer, wasn't a job that Tanzil took lightly, though it wasn't a job he did in accordance with the established laws and guidelines of the US Fish and Wildlife Service. He had personal reasons for choosing this profession. It allowed him the freedom to protect his kind—bear shifters—from the humans who employed him.

The tenets of his job put him in charge of thousands of square miles of forests, lakes, and rivers. He was responsible for everything from the trees and water to the creatures that inhabited these lands.

And he was responsible for keeping humans out of this pristine wilderness.

Humans might call him "warden" as a job title, but bears used that moniker to honor his status as one of the few responsible for the care and upkeep of the wards protecting shifters from being detected by those who would harm them—humans. Of course, even in the bear community, the idea of a Warden was a well-kept secret. The last thing they needed was for knowledge of this special kind of bear shifter to get out. Humans would hunt them down and eliminate them.

The vastness of his domain meant sometimes certain parts weren't checked out with regularity. Today he visited the short-term parking lot about an hour outside of Bear's Cove where he'd encountered the comely Logan Fordline a week ago. Sometimes city folk liked to camp here. A few of them would even shift into bear form and wander for a day or two. Seeing as how they were from the city, they didn't stay in the wild for very long. Many of them had a romanticized notion that remaining in bear form for weeks on end meant a special kind of freedom.

They found out pretty quickly it was a harsh existence that required them to constantly search for food. And, because bears were solitary creatures, it tended to be a lonely existence as well. In human form, bear shifters were gregarious creatures. It was folly to think it was natural to remain in one form or the other all the time. Shifters needed time as both in order to feel complete.

Tanzil checked his records, noting the dark blue pickup truck in the lot was the same one that had been there five days before. Given how inexperienced Logan had seemed, Tanzil hadn't expected to see the car still there. He peeked into the bed to find camping gear still neatly stowed, food and clothing locked tight in the cab.

Warning bells sounded in his head. No shifter who'd grown up in mostly human form could tolerate remaining in bear form for so long. There was a decent chance Fordline was lost or injured, and it was Tanzil's responsibility to find him.

Using his radio meant reminding his fellow game wardens of his existence. Part of the magic of the wards he enforced meant those outside the wards forgot about everything inside them. Oh, they knew there were hundreds of miles of virgin forest there, and they knew several villages, townships, small cities, and brief hamlets could be found there, but they never came looking for them.

Never.

Contacting them meant they'd remember he was there. They'd remember he could respond to calls as well as any other warden. Within a week, they'd forget again, but until then, they'd be a thorn in his side.

He decided to investigate before calling to see if a report had been filed outside the perimeter of the wards. Perhaps if he couldn't pick up the scent of the roaming bear, he could phone Cord Bearsmith, the Sheriff of Bear's Cove, to run a check. But that would also become a pain in his ass that wouldn't subside after a week. Being a bear and being inside the wards, Cord would remember to pester him.

Not that he didn't do it already. Cord's husband, Brock, was kind of related to him.

With a sigh, Tanzil stripped out of his clothes. He folded them neatly, and then he rolled them into tiny bundles he could slip into a sack. When he had everything the way he wanted, he added his car keys and his gun to the pack. Then he positioned it on his back with the cord loose on his torso. Once he shifted, the cord would tighten, and the pack would travel with him.

This was one of his favorite inventions, and a wave of sadness washed through him as he thought about the person who'd made the backpack for him. He breathed through it, and then he focused on the task at hand. The owner of the truck needed to be found.

He unpacked items of clothing from the frame pack in the back of Fordline's truck, sniffed them to get the scent in his nose, and then he shoved them in his bag.

Shifting, he felt the straps of the pack tighten around his torso perfectly. Then he sniffed around the perimeter, searching for the barest trace of an odor. Bears were known for their great sense of smell, and Tanzil's tracking skills, enhanced by his status as a Warden, were second to none. It took some time, but he picked up the scent.

For most of the day, he followed bits and pieces of scent, finding markings every now and again to confirm that he was on the right track. Many hours later, he found himself on the edge of the wards. Rocky terrain marked the border. This area wasn't popular with humans. In the distance, the rocks became boulders until the sheer face of a cliff rose in the distance. On top of that cliff was grazing land, farm land, and a few miles away, a village.

He shifted to human form and looked around. The trail came to an abrupt halt, and that was never a good thing. Tanzil closed his eyes and exhaled. Then he dressed himself and examined the area for evidence.

It didn't take long to find drag marks. Brown bears were large, and they weren't easy to move. Dragging this bear had ripped up grasses, and there were deep gouges and tire tracks in the ground about fifteen feet away.

Tanzil fought the flashbacks, but they flooded to him anyway. With a ragged cry, he leaned against a tree and let them wash through his mind. At times like this, moments were precious, but Tanzil knew it was better to work with his trauma than against it.

He'd come home from a long few days at work. Sometimes as a game warden, his assignment was so far away from home that he camped out or stayed overnight in a ranger station. The hour was still early, so Tanzil had come into the house quietly because he knew Namir liked to sleep in.

Only Namir hadn't been asleep. He'd met Tanzil at the front door, a huge smile splitting his face. *Guess what? I'm pregnant. Twins.*

Joy had leaped through Tanzil's heart. They'd made love, napped, and made love some more. The next day, they'd shifted to go for a romp in the woods surrounding their home. Flashes of horror and feelings of helplessness assailed Tanzil. He heard the loud report and felt the searing heat of bullets penetrating his thick hide. Namir's screams followed him into unconsciousness. When he woke, he found himself in a hospital in Bear's Cove.

Surgeons had removed the bullets, and Namir was nowhere to be found. Cord Bearsmith, who'd been a deputy at the time, told him that the scent trail for Namir had stopped at a clearing, and they'd been unable to locate Namir. Tanzil left the hospital, ignoring the doctors and nurses who tried to stop him. It took him three days, but he found Namir—his pregnant husband—in a cage hidden near the woods behind a ramshackle cabin.

His prone form, still bear-shaped, lay unmoving in a corner of the cage. The odor of blood permeated the air, and he knew that he'd lost everything. Back when he'd first become a conservation officer, Bear Elders had offered him a chance to also train as a Warden, but he'd turned them down. At the time, he'd been young, and he'd just met Namir. The idea of going away for a whole year to be trained had not interested a young bear in love.

Tanzil had never recovered from losing his family, and with them, his dreams. When they'd offered again to train him as a Warden, he'd thrown himself into the grueling training that taught him to harness the energy of the Mists to protect his kind. Now he focused on the job that had become his calling, and nothing else.

Tanzil shook his head to clear away that last image, even as he used it to fortify himself for the next task. Another bear had been taken.

He went back to the border and closed his eyes to expand his senses. The wards were still intact, though evidence of tampering showed humans had penetrated the mists. Wards didn't keep humans out as much as they prevented them from wanting to come this way. But a determined human could get in, and sometimes a wayward one wandered through. The wayward ones didn't worry Tanzil, but the determined ones—they never had good intentions.

Whispering a few mystical words, Tanzil called forth the memory of the mist to point the way. A red SUV. An open-topped trailer with wooden sides. Tarp. Rope. Two men.

Tanzil opened his eyes. He had a visual, and now he needed to find his prey.

He packed up his sack, shifted to bear form, and returned to his vehicle. Night had fallen by the time he made it there, but he had a mission, and nothing deterred him from a mission.

Back at his truck, he placed a call to the Sheriff's office at Bear's Cove.

"Bearsmith." Cord Bearsmith was now the sheriff, which put him in charge of Bear's Cove and the surrounding area.

"Hi Cord. This is Tanzil Jareth." Including his last name wasn't necessary, but he did it anyway.

"Tanzil, buddy, how are you?" Cord's neutral tone warmed, welcoming him even though Tanzil never called for reasons other than business. This time was no different.

"I got a pickup truck that's been sitting here for five days. I think the owner is Logan Fordline. Can you run a search to see if Logan has been reported missing, or if he's been found anywhere?" Tanzil swallowed back a small twinge. Before Namir had been taken from him, he'd socialized with friends and family in Bear's Cove, including

Cord, who was married to Namir's cousin, Brock. Since then, he'd withdrawn, and now he led a solitary existence, which suited him just fine.

"Sure. Logan went up about eight days ago. What makes you think he's in trouble?" Cord's wariness came through, loud and clear.

Eight days? He'd promised to return in five. Damn. Sometimes the days blended together, and he forgot changes to his routine. What if Fordline had returned, and Tanzil hadn't been there?

Memories of sky blue eyes, flashes of a flirty smile, and images of those kissable lips assailed him. Then he swallowed down the doubt niggling in his gut. Nothing in the truck had been touched since he'd been there last. Tanzil's instincts were consistently good, and his use of magic had confirmed his suspicions. These were not things he would explain to anyone. "I just know." He cleared his throat. "I need you to run another search for me."

This time, he described the truck and the two men from his vision. He knew the chances of finding them immediately were slim, but this was merely the beginning of his search.

"I've got a couple of possibilities for the truck." Cord rattled off three addresses, all outside the wards. "Are you going to call in outside help?"

"Nope." Protecting the bear settlements came first. Including outsiders meant limiting his search, and it could endanger a bear's life. "I'll call when I have news."

"Tanzil?" Cord called out just before Tanzil ended the call.

"Go ahead." He struggled not to growl. Not only did he want to get going on his mission, but he didn't want to hear anything Cord had to say.

"How about, when you bring Logan back to Bear's Cove, you come over for dinner? We miss you. Brock can make that quiche you like so much"

Tanzil squeezed the bridge of his nose. Before Namir's death, the four of them used to hang out regularly. "We'll see." He wanted to refuse outright, but Cord would have kept him on the phone longer to try to change his mind. This way he could focus on the thing that mattered right now—returning Logan Fordline to his loved ones. "Jareth out."

No lights shone through the windows, and nobody answered the door at the first address. The night was dark, but a full moon rose above the trees, making up for the fact there were no streetlights. The house had an empty feel, so Tanzil poked around outside. He used his nose more than his eyes, but he didn't catch the scent of bear.

Next door, a family sat around a fire pit, roasting marshmallows and hot dogs. Tanzil approached the fence. "Good evening. I'm Tanzil Jareth, Fish and Wildlife Service. I was looking for Chad and Emily McConnell. Have you seen them around?"

"They're not home, officer." A barrel-shaped man limped across the next yard over. "Can I help you with something?"

Since he'd already determined that no bear was in the vicinity, Tanzil was ready to move onto the next location on his list. "Do the people who live here own a red SUV?"

Barrel-man nodded. "They left three or four days ago to go visit relatives in North Carolina. My son is picking up the mail and watering the plants while they're gone."

Tanzil did one last visual sweep. "Do they have a trailer for the SUV?"

The guy scratched his chin. "Not that I've ever seen. Is there a problem? You want me to call them for you?"

Something here didn't sit right with Tanzil, though he couldn't pinpoint the exact cause of his unease. "That's not necessary. I received a complaint about a red SUV with a trailer, but if your friends are halfway across the country, it couldn't have been them." Tanzil shook hands with the man. "You have a good day."

The next address had a red SUV parked in the driveway, but the older model was larger and darker, so it wasn't the one from Tanzil's vision.

One perk of searching so late in the evening meant most people would be home. The last address was a house at the end of a long driveway. Trees surrounded the area, making ruts in the twin dirt tracks difficult to discern. Tanzil drove slowly, his vehicle rocking precariously at every pothole.

The house at the end of the road ended up being a tiny cabin. Next to it was a red SUV that had seen better days. This was not the car the mists had shown to him. Before he could turn around and leave, the front door flew open. Light filtered from behind to show the outline of a woman with a child perched on one hip and a pistol in her other hand.

Tanzil parked so she could see the emblem on the side of his truck that identified him a member of law enforcement, though if she was one of those crazies who distrusted law enforcement, then his action might have no effect.

Of course, having been shot before, he had no patience for useless fear. He also figured the child meant she was in a protective mode, not an offensive one.

20

He emerged from the truck. "Good evening, ma'am. I'm Tanzil Jareth, Fish and Wildlife Service. How are you?"

She lowered the weapon. "Hi, officer. I wasn't expecting company."

"It is late," he acknowledged. "I'm sorry for disturbing you. I'm following up on a report concerning a red SUV, but I can see that yours is not the one I'm looking for." He looked her up and down, noting the tension and fatigue in the lines of her body. Then he glanced around, opening up his senses. "Are you okay, ma'am?"

"Since you're not my ex-husband, I'm fine."

That explained the greeting. He pressed his lips together. Part of him wanted to counsel her on better ways to confront an angry ex, but most of him wanted to leave human problems to humans so he could find Logan Fordline. But the protective side of him, the side that had gone into this profession in the first place, asserted itself.

He approached the front door. "You're afraid of him?"

She nodded, a brief, curt move.

"What did you say your name was?"

"Inez Hendricks."

"It's nice to meet you, Ms. Hendricks. Does your ex-husband know you're here?"

"No, but some friends do, and he's good at sweet-talking, so one of them might slip up and tell him where I am. He doesn't know about this place. It belongs to my grandfather, and he only uses it during deer hunting season."

Tanzil had no patience for a man who mistreated those he was supposed to love. He couldn't see how someone could fail to treasure his lover and child. His heart ached anew at the memory of his loss. He handed her a card with his name and number on it. "Feel free to call if he shows up."

She took it, a wariness in her eyes betraying her true feelings. She was a prisoner, caged by fear and circumstance, and she didn't trust any hand reaching out to help her.

"I mean it," he said gently. "I'm stationed closer than the deputy outpost. I can be here faster."

He left there, restless because he'd ruled out two of the three possibilities. Now he needed to follow up on the McConnells' whereabouts. He went out to the main road and called Cord again. "Can you run a check on Chad and Emily McConnell? Do they have other properties listed?"

"Who is this?" A voice that wasn't Cord's answered.

"Warden Tanzil Jareth. Where is Cord?"

The man's tone thawed. "He's gone home for the night. This is Deputy Dak Freeman. How can I help you tonight, Warden?"

"I found a truck belonging to Logan Fordline. He appears to be missing, so I'm following up some leads to look for him. Can you run that check for me?"

"Logan Fordline?" Deputy Freeman's pitch rose with worry. "Logan's missing? How do you know?"

He exhaled. "It's my job to know."

The other end went silent. "I'm from Forrest Hills, so I know about Wardens." He emphasized 'wardens' to let Tanzil know he was aware of trade secrets.

"That's great. Please run the check on Chad and Emily McConnell."

"Cord did that. I'm looking at a report from five days ago about a bear attack on Chad McConnell. I'll call the officer who filed the report to see what I can find out."

Tanzil closed his eyes. If Logan had attacked Chad, then there had been a reason behind it. Bears didn't attack without reason, and shifters required even more reason. "What else does the report say?"

"It's bare-bones. McConnell reported startling a female bear with two cubs. She took a swipe at him before running away with her cubs." Freeman snorted. "There is so much wrong with this story, I don't even know where to begin. Obviously the officer in charge had no fucking clue about bears."

"Yeah," Tanzil agreed. Bears—the regular kind, not shifters—were preparing to hibernate. Cubs would be older and able to hide, and they'd all be more interested in eating than in confronting some idiot out for a walk in the woods. "What hospital? I'd like to talk with McConnell myself."

"Do you want backup? Logan is a friend of mine. I'm willing to do whatever it takes to bring him home safely."

Tanzil preferred to work alone. "How about you talk to the officer who took the report, and run a deeper check on the McConnells, and send me anything you find? That would be very helpful."

"Sure. Call if anything changes. I'll send you my cell number in case you need it."

"Sounds good." Tanzil ended the call and headed to the hospital.

They wouldn't let him in to see Chad McConnell. "He's asleep," a female nurse explained. "And he's in the Intensive Care Unit. Only immediate family can visit."

Tanzil scowled. He hadn't come for a fucking visit; he'd come to grill the man on his alleged encounter. "This a matter of some urgency concerning a missing person. I need to speak with Mr. McConnell right now."

"Let me call the doctor."

This was not proceeding as smoothly as it should, but Tanzil had no choice. He waited.

An hour later, he left the hospital with nothing. McConnell had been half out of his mind with fever. He'd contracted an additional virus since he'd come to the hospital, and his faculties had deserted him.

But Tanzil had detected the scent of bear on the man, which was confirmation enough. He called Deputy Freeman as soon as he got into his car. "Fordline's scent was on McConnell." Now he had to find what the bastard had done with the shifter. "Have you located the wife?"

Freeman cleared his throat. "No. I found her parents in North Carolina, but they say they haven't seen or heard from Emily or Chad in over a week. Chad has a brother, Jared, who lives out that way. I tried calling, but the phone goes straight to voicemail. I'm sending you the address right now."

The address wasn't far from the property where the woman hiding from her ex-husband lived. Tanzil found himself once again traveling that winding mountain road. He passed the rutted driveway separating Inez Hendricks from certain doom. Distances were relative out in the wilderness, and so he traveled for another hour before reaching his destination. Darkness had fallen over the land, and Tanzil's sense of urgency increased by the minute.

A narrow dirt driveway, this one in better shape than Inez's, meandered next to a stream for a ways before diverging. It terminated in a clearing featuring another of those ubiquitous hunting cabins, but this one had a red SUV parked near the front door. Tanzil pulled up behind it, but one car couldn't box in another without help for the other three sides. The house provided one blockade, but that left two open sides.

Before he could emerge from his car, a man jumped into the red SUV. He gunned the engine, sending dust and dirt flying, and he took off.

More than apprehending that asshole, Tanzil needed to check for signs of Logan. He needed to know if he'd made it on time, or if he was too late—just as he'd been too late to save Namir. He let Jared McConnell flee. If he needed to, he could catch up with him later.

Tanzil alighted from his truck and knocked on the door. "Game Warden," he called. "Is anyone inside?"

No answer.

"I'm coming in."

Gun drawn, he opened the door. The cabin was tiny. The main room had a small kitchenette, a sofa with the bed folded out, and a television. Off to the right, a closet-sized bedroom had a full mattress on the floor. An opened suitcase sat next to it, the contents in disarray, and an electric cattle prod was propped against the wall behind it.

The final room was a bathroom with a shower stall and toilet, but no sink.

With the house clear, he went out the back door, and the sight he'd dreaded greeted him.

A metal cage occupied one corner of the yard. He eyed a ramshackle shed warily as he hurried over to the enclosure and shined his flashlight inside. It illuminated two creatures. The bear was in rough shape. Thin and shaking, blood and pus seeped from a long gouge on his side.

The other denizen was a woman. She slept nestled against the bear, probably for warmth, and she didn't stir as he approached. Bruises mottled her eye and shoulder, which is all he could see because clothing covered the rest of her. She'd bled from the blow to her face. Tanzil sniffed, but he didn't detect that she was a shifter. She simply smelled human.

Examining the cage, he noted the padlock. He reached through the bars and shook the woman's shoulder. "Miss?"

She started awake, a small shriek escaping as she jerked away.

Tanzil held up a hand. "It's okay. I'm a conservation officer. Where is the key so I can unlock the cage?"

She glanced around. "Jared?"

"He lit out of here when I pulled up."

Her eyes dulled. "He has the key.

"What's your name?"

"Emily McConnell. Jared is my brother-in-law."

"What are your injuries?" He asked her, but his gaze remained on the bear. He was certain it was Logan, but he didn't want to tip his hand, not in front of a human.

"Jared hit me with the butt of his gun, and then he locked me in here." She hugged her arms around her body and shivered. "The bear is harmless. He's—um—he's a pet."

Flashes of the good-looking young man with startling blue eyes he'd met bombarded his brain. Logan was no pet. Fury made Tanzil's voice harsh. "He's been shot. Starved. Mistreated. It's illegal to keep a bear as a pet, and it's immoral to treat anyone or anything like this."

She blinked, her eyes a little unfocused.

24

"I'm going to get bolt cutters out of my truck, and I'm going to call an ambulance for you."

Really he wanted to call one for Fordline, but he couldn't because he wasn't in bear country. This was yet another reason for bears to stay inside the fucking wards. He called for an ambulance, and then he called Deputy Freeman as he rummaged for bolt cutters.

"I think I found him. He's badly hurt. I'm going to load him into my truck and bring him to Bear's Cove Hospital."

Freeman exhaled. "You're five hours out, minimum, and there's a wicked storm heading your way. It's already here, and we've lost power to half the city. The MedEvac can't go out in a storm like this, or else I'd send it."

Tanzil sniffed the air, but he detected no sign of rain. Clouds blocked the stars and the full moon he'd witnessed earlier, but that didn't necessarily mean rain. "He's in ursine form. I can't take him to a human hospital. Assholes won't treat him. There's a woman here as well. I called an ambulance for her. I'll call you back once I'm closer to Bear's Cove."

Though it was far away, there was nowhere else to take him. Forrest Hills was only two hours away, but they didn't have the medical facilities or a helicopter. They needed to get a fucking helicopter in the border lands.

He returned to the cage.

Emily tried to stand, but she fell over, crashing into Fordline.

The bear whimpered, and one eye opened. It glanced around and stopped on Tanzil, where it took a minute to focus. "It's okay, buddy. Nobody's going to hurt you."

A low growl issued from the bear.

Emily used the bars to get to her feet. "That's what I keep telling him, too."

Okay, so that assurance had a negative connotation to Fordline in his current condition. Tanzil tried a different tactic. "I'm going to get you out of here. I'll take you to the hospital, and they'll fix you up, good as new."

"The vet, you mean." Emily seemed stronger, and she narrowed her eyes at Tanzil.

He hated that term. Vets were for animals. Shifters had a wild side, but they were natural, sentient beings with a very human side. "Animal hospital."

"You called animal control?" There was an edge to her voice. For someone who'd been beaten and thrust into a cage with a bear, she was awfully defiant.

"I'm animal control." It was official. He did not like Emily. He cut through the bolt and opened the cage. He held an arm out to Emily. "Can you walk, or do you need me to carry you?"

She leaned heavily on him as she hobbled out of the cage. He scooped her up and carried her to the house, not from any sense of gallantry, but because he wanted to get her away from the bear—for the bear's safety—as quickly as possible. Even petite humans with bruises on their face weren't necessarily safe, though he doubted she was responsible for this mess. Being beaten and locked up spoke volumes for the choices she'd been allowed to make with her life.

But he'd met abused humans before. Many of them stubbornly stuck by their abusers, and he wasn't willing to risk Fordline's life over it.

He took her inside the house and set her on the folded-out sofa in the living room. "Let's get your face cleaned up so I can see what we're dealing with." Though he wanted to attend to the bear, he forced himself to see to Emily's wounds. "Talk me through what happened. You said this was your brother-in-law's house. How did you come to be here?"

"Jared and Chad, that's my husband, got a bear as a pet. So we came up here to help train it, but then it attacked Chad, and now he's in the hospital, and Jared got mad at me for it. He hit me and locked me in there."

Given the stench of the woman's clothes and her general state of dishabille, Tanzil estimated that she'd been in the cage for over a day. "How long were you kept in there?"

"Two days. It's so cold out, especially at night." She wrapped a blanket around her body. "I'm so cold."

"You're okay now." He rose. "I'm going to check on the bear."

She frowned. "You know what he is—don't you? Of course, a game warden would know that these hills are infested with bear shifters."

Tanzil forced his face to remain impassive. "I'm no doctor, but I think you have a concussion. Stay put. I'll be back in a few minutes."

He went outside, fully aware that Emily was likely watching his actions. The bear didn't stir as he approached the cage. Ducking inside, he crouched down next to the injured shifter, and he set a hand on Fordline's shoulder, and the bear flinched. "Logan, my name is Tanzil Jareth. In case you don't remember, we met a few days ago. I've come here to rescue you."

The bear opened his eyes, but he didn't move.

Tanzil noted the shallow, pained breathing. "You've been shot, and you've lost a lot of blood. I'm going to need you to shift so I can get you into my car. I'll take you to a hospital in Bear's Cove where they know how to treat a shifter properly."

His eyes drifted closed.

"Logan, wake up. Keep your eyes open. It's very important to stay awake right now." Tanzil didn't know if that was true, but every time Fordline closed his eyes, Tanzil worried that he'd never wake up again.

Logan opened his eyes, and he glanced toward the cabin, worry furrowing his ursine brow.

"Yes, I know there's a human around, but if I'm going to charge her with kidnapping and torture, I need you to be in your human form. With you as a bear, it's a far lesser charge, a slap on the wrist." Tanzil scowled. "We can't let these people get away with what they did to you."

At best, Logan seemed unconvinced. He closed his eyes.

Tanzil needed to approach this differently. He had no idea how long Fordline had been held there or what they'd done to him. That cattle prod probably had been used more than once. "Don't move. I'll be right back."

As he rummaged in the storage box in the rear of his truck, Emily came out the front door.

Still wrapped in a blanket, she sat on the stoop and regarded him through shrewd eyes. "You're going to have to put it down."

"Excuse me?" He longed to snatch the blanket around her and take it to Fordline.

"The bear. He was in sad shape when I got here. I haven't been able to get him to do anything, and he hasn't moved in at least three days."

"How long has he been in there?"

She shrugged. "A little over a week, I think."

"Where did he get the bear?"

"I don't know. Chad and him come up here to drink beer and maybe get a deer. It was in the cage when I got here."

Tanzil found the warm blanket for which he'd been searching. "Capturing wild bears is a felony."

"Hunting them ain't, and Chad and Jared both got a license to get one."

White-hot rage had him out of the back of the truck and on the step in the blink of an eye. He loomed over her. "That's not hunting. Animal cruelty is a crime as well, Mrs. McConnell, and if I find out you took part in this travesty, then rest assured that I will charge you accordingly."

"I was locked in there, asshole. I'm the victim."

He pointed to the door. "Stay inside until the ambulance gets here. It's going to take at least an hour." He could have called for a MedEvac for her, but he didn't think her injuries were that severe.

Without waiting, he went around back. Inside the cage, Fordline shivered. He covered the bear with the blanket, and then he leaned down. "You're hidden from view. Shift, Logan. Shift so I can see full extent of your injuries. Shift so I can charge these people with everything they have coming to them."

The lump underneath the dark blanket changed shape, and now it shivered violently. Tanzil lifted the blanket and used his flashlight to check the damage. Now that the fur was gone, he noted how the bullet had grazed his side.

"The good news is you won't need surgery." His attempt at a smile fell flat as he noted the blood coating Fordline's skin and pooling on the floor. Pus seeped from the wound. "I think. Can you talk?"

Fordline's eyes closed, and the man passed out.

"Fuck," Tanzil muttered. "This is not good." He scooped Logan up and carried him to his truck.

Emily waited with her back against the door and a Glock in her hand.

He should have searched the luggage.

"Where do you think you're going?" She waved her hand at Logan. "I knew he was a bear shifter. Put him down, warden. He stays."

With his hands full, he couldn't adequately defend either of them. Tanzil gently set Logan on the ground, making sure the blanket stayed underneath to give some protection from the damp and the chill.

"Now step away from him." Emily motioned to the side. "I'm sorry about this, Warden, I truly am, but I can't have you messing up my dream."

"Your dream?" He lifted his hands to show they were empty. "What dream?"

"I'm going to charge a hundred bucks a head for people to see a real, live bear shifter, and when he's no longer attracting a crowd, well—he's worth more dead than alive."

This was not Tanzil's first time being held at gunpoint. He relied on his preternatural reflexes and his training to give him the edge over a woman whose eyes failed to focus because she had a concussion and she'd been exposed to the elements. He leaped, taking her down before her tiny human brain could process the action.

28

In the distance, he heard the sounds of engines and tires.

He shoved Emily's gun out of reach and handcuffed her. The ambulance and a sheriff's car arrived. Light flooded the place.

"Over here," he called. "I think she has a concussion."

"Why is she handcuffed?"

Tanzil went over to Logan as he answered the deputy's question. "She pulled a gun on me. It looks like she and her brother-in-law, Jared McConnell, kidnapped and tortured this man. McConnell took off when I got here. He's in a red SUV. I have the make, model, and plate number in my car.

The EMT paused, kit in hand, and he looked between the two bodies on the ground. "Who is first?"

As much as he didn't want a human seeing to Logan, he knew the cub needed help, and he knew that Deputy Freeman had been correct—five hours was too long to wait for medical care. Tanzil motioned to the man at his feet. "This guy."

The EMT knelt next to Logan and peered into his face. He peeled Logan's eyes open and shined a light to check his pupil response.

Logan flinched, jerking his head back and blinking rapidly.

"It's okay, sir. My name is Henry. I'm an EMT. Can you tell me your name?"

While Henry worked on Logan, the ambulance driver saw to Emily's wounds.

Tanzil extended a hand to the deputy. "I'm Tanzil Jareth, conservation officer."

The deputy shook his hand. "You must be new around these parts. I'm Deputy Ian Glover. Nice to meet you. What brought you out here?"

"Missing person report."

While keeping an eye on the injured shifter, he proceeded to fill in the deputy on most of what had transpired.

Chapter 3

Logan

Everything hurt. From the roots of his teeth to the marrow in his bones, pain of both the sharp and dull varieties shot through his body.

"Gunshot wound." The medic had opened his blanket, exposing Logan's naked body to the elements. In the distance, he heard the authoritative voice of the shifter who'd saved him.

Logan didn't want some strange human poking around while he was in this vulnerable state. Had the man told Logan his name? If so, Logan couldn't recall, though the man seemed somehow familiar. The only thing he remembered was his job title. "Warden." The word whispered from his parched lips.

"What's that?" The EMT leaned closer. He'd said his name, but Logan could barely think enough to remember to breathe.

"Warden."

"You want the warden?"

"Yes." The world swam in and out of focus. The next thing he knew, brown filled his field of vision—large, brown eyes, dark brown hair, and even brown skin. The man exuded power and authority. Using all his strength, he grasped for the Warden. "Don't leave me."

"You're in good hands." Warden's warm, strong hands closed around Logan's. "I promise."

Desperate, Logan gripped Warden as tightly as he could. "Don't leave. Please."

Those hard brown eyes softened. "I'm not going anywhere."

The edges of the world faded, and Logan felt his consciousness flow toward the black spots. "Bear's Cove—you said."

The man nodded. "I'm going to let these gentlemen get you stabilized, and then I'll take you home. You have my word."

Warden might have said more, but Logan didn't hear it.

The next time he became aware of his surroundings, he found himself asleep in the passenger seat of a truck. The reclined position put a crick in his neck, but it was a far sight better than sleeping naked on the ground.

He opened his eyes to find no real difference. Blurry lights came into focus, and he recognized the light from dashboard controls. He moved his head, and a whimper escaped.

A hand brushed his arm. "Shhh. It's okay, Logan. The nightmare is over."

He stirred again, and something on his other arm burned.

"Try not to move your arm, okay? You have an IV in it, and I don't know how to take it out or fix it if you knock it around."

That explained why he didn't feel so dehydrated, and also why he had to pee so badly. "Warden?"

"That's me. I'm taking you to Bear's Cove Hospital like I promised. We're about four hours out. Maybe five."

"Have to pee."

Warden chuckled. "Somehow I knew that was coming."

The speed of the vehicle decreased, and they stopped in the road. Logan reached for his seat belt, but he didn't have the coordination to make the connection.

"Stay put, cub. It's raining buckets outside. Normally I wouldn't let that stop you, but you're naked and I'm not convinced you have the strength to stand on your own two feet." Warden undid his seat belt and handed over a paper cup. "Sorry, but this is going to have to suffice."

Long past the point of humiliation, Logan let Warden scoot him into a better position. There were worse things in life than having a handsome warden help him urinate. Chase was going to lose his shit laughing when Logan told him about this part. Maybe he'd emphasize it in order to detract from the rest—because there was no way in hell he was ever going to talk about anything that happened to him in that hellhole.

Warden disposed of everything, and then they were on their way. Logan wanted to stay awake. He wanted to talk to the man who'd rescued him, but his lips wouldn't work, and he was so fucking tired.

Minutes later, the car stopped again, waking Logan. Outside the windshield, rain battered the vehicle so hard it was impossible to see more than a few inches. Being out in this would have killed him. He was thankful to have been rescued before this deluge opened up. He wanted to say those things to Warden, but his eyelids were too heavy. They wouldn't stay open.

Warden shouted into the radio, his voice a single anchor that kept Logan from drifting off again.

"The bridge at Ore Creek is out?"

The voice on the radio cut in and out, but most of his message came through. "Affirmative. I'm looking at alternate routes, but there's flooding all over. Is there a ranger station nearby?"

Warden exhaled an aggravated breath. "Affirmative. I'll find shelter immediately."

The radio let out a high-pitched squeal, and then only static came through.

"Looks like we lost a tower. Okay, change of plans. Fuck. I'm sorry, Logan, but we're going to have to wait out the storm before I can get you to the hospital."

As long as he was with Warden, Logan knew he was safe. He gave in and went back to sleep.

It seemed like a minute had passed when his eyes flew open. Pellets of water thundered from the sky, pummeling the roof of the truck. The noise was deafening. Lightning flashed, and thunder shook the ground, but the rain made it impossible to hear.

And Warden was gone.

Alone in the truck, Logan wondered where they were. Through sheets of rain, he made out a structure with light blazing from one window and a light on the porch. He realized that Warden must have found a cabin.

The passenger door opened, and the deluge drenched the blanket. Logan shivered and tried to turn his body. There was no way he was getting from point A to point B without a thorough soaking.

Warden shouted something, but his voice disappeared into the maelstrom. He set a clear bag on Logan's lap, scooped Logan in his arms, and ran with him to the cover of the porch.

Well, maybe during a typical storm, the porch would provide cover. During this storm, that wasn't happening. Rain pummeled them with amazing force. Warden moved quickly, getting them both into the cabin.

The inside was cozy. Logan had a second to process in the dim light from the hurricane lantern, and then he realized the wetness coating the inside of his blanket was sticky.

Warden unwrapped the sodden blanket and set him on the sofa. "This'll do until I get the generator going. I'm sure you'll want a shower and some fresh clothes." His mouth opened as if he'd meant to say more, but instead he gaped at the crimson water dripping from the blanket. "You're bleeding."

Rivulets of blood ran down his arm, leaking from where the IV needle had torn from his skin. The sight of blood had never been on the list of Logan's favorite things. His head felt cottony, and he had the sensation of floating above his body.

He saw Warden lay him down and put pressure on the wound. Warden's lips moved, but Logan didn't hear the words. The man lying on the black leather sofa was pale and skinny, his body and his sodden hair streaked with filth. He had a gash along one side, stretching from the front side of his right hip, over his ass, and up his side. The straight line on his ursine form had turned to a weird, meandering path on his human self.

Wait—that man looked nothing like Logan. Logan Fordline was clean and well-dressed. Even when his hair was messy, it was the sexy kind of messy achieved after a lot of time spent styling it. His body was healthy and strong, not this emaciated lump.

The foggy part of his brain refused to let anything process. Eventually it carried him away.

Tanzil

He kept passing out. Tanzil didn't know what to make of it. The EMT hadn't been trained in treating trauma. After much arguing, he agreed to hang the IV bag in Tanzil's truck and let Tanzil drive Logan to the hospital in Bear's Cove. He'd repeated several times that Logan needed urgent medical care.

But he hadn't told Tanzil what to do in case the fucking storm of the century came through, washing out roads and bridges and making driving generally impossible.

He hadn't told Tanzil what to do if he was forced to take Logan to his place instead of a hospital.

While Tanzil had basic first aid training, nothing had prepared him for this. Logan couldn't even go to the bathroom without help.

Okay, maybe that was an easy one. But the rip in his arm gushing blood—that was a new one. Tanzil kept a firm pressure on it, but he needed a clone to go into the bathroom and get bandages, antiseptic, gauze, and whatever else one put on a gaping wound.

With one hand, he kept pressure on Logan's arm. With the other, he unbuttoned his shirt. The thing was wet with rain and blood, but it would have to do for now. It took some one-handed wrangling but he wrapped it around Logan's arm. Then he sprinted for the bathroom.

He made it behind the sofa before he tripped and fell, face-first, to the floor. Fucking area rug. He hated it. He'd always hated it. But Namir had put it in the entryway separating the large living room into two halves, and so Tanzil left it in place.

Scrambling to his feet, Tanzil sprinted the rest of the way to the storage closet in the first-floor bathroom with all the first aid supplies. Living alone in the middle of nowhere, he had more than the basics. He returned to find Logan hadn't moved. His chest rose and fell with shallow breaths, and his skin was flushed.

"Fever. Fucking great." He knelt next to the sofa and tended to Logan's arm. "You'd better not die on me, cub."

After he got that squared away, he covered Logan up, and then he took care of himself. No power meant water was at a premium, and a warm shower was out of the question. Ironically, buckets poured from the sky. His rain barrels were no doubt overflowing.

He dried off and threw on warm clothes.

Then he set about figuring out how to clean his dirty charge. Filth caked every inch of Logan's body. In addition to the wound from the bullet grazing his thick hide, Logan had marks from the cattle prod, cuts and contusions all over, and a million bug bites. Tanzil hoped Logan hadn't picked up fleas or lice.

He got a fire going in the large stone fireplace that took up a whole corner of the front room. In addition to heating up the place, it provided necessary light. Once that was roaring, he threw down a bunch of old, clean towels next to the front door, donned rain gear, and took three buckets outside. First he used the rain to clean them out, then he wiped the inside of one down with rubbing alcohol before filling it with fresh water.

He set the buckets on the towels and took off his wet slicker.

"Okay, Logan. It's time for a bath. I have to warn you—I've never done this to a sleeping person before, and I'll apologize in advance for anything I do wrong."

He eyed the injured man sleeping on his sofa, and shook his head. Water was going to get everywhere. This needed to be done in a bathroom. Then he glanced at the source of warmth and light.

Or, he could do it on the flagstones surrounding the fireplace. They were designed by Mother Nature herself to weather any storm.

So he gently lifted Logan, blanket and all, and placed him in front of the fireplace. Then he opened the blanket. It would serve for padding and water-collection. Already blood-soaked and dirty from holding his charge, it was destined for the trash anyway.

He started with the torso. The dirt was so thick that Tanzil was surprised to see such pale skin once the dried-on mud fell away. He worked slowly, pausing to murmur soothing words whenever Logan whimpered.

When he finished, he eyeballed Logan's hair. Matted into clumps, Tanzil knew there was no way it was coming out. Using the last of the charge in his electric razor, he shaved Logan's head, leaving him with a half-inch of hair. That was much easier to clean.

Perhaps the younger bear would be pissed when he realized what Tanzil had done. Or maybe he'd just be happy to be alive.

Now that Logan was clean, the blanket under him was as sodden as the one he'd dropped at the front door. Tanzil lifted Logan and took him back to the sofa.

"Forgot a fresh blanket." He left Logan on the sofa while he went to the closet in the main hall that held extra linen. When he returned, he looked over his handiwork.

Logan had the long, lithe build of an omega and the chiseled body of a man who took care of himself. "You clean up nicely," he said before he caught himself. "Do not ogle the injured, passed-out victim."

He wrapped Logan in a soft comforter, and then he settled down in his comfortable, old recliner, where he fell asleep.

Chapter 4—Logan

A cold shoulder pulled Logan from a deep sleep. He tried to move his arm, intending to tug the fallen covers back in place, but his limbs were too heavy. Something was holding him down.

Chill turned to panic, and he cried out, his eyes flying open as he struggled against his bonds.

"Shhh. It's okay. The nightmare is over. You're safe." A hand stroked his hair away from his face, the gentle touch not at all like the condescending petting his captor had done.

The voice came from outside his field of vision. Logan tried to twist around, but he couldn't move. "Who the hell are you? Where am I? What did you do to me?" In his mind, the questions poured forth, demanding and firm. In reality, his tongue stumbled over most of the words, slurring away anything that might be construed as firm.

Something squeaked, and the man who'd spoken came into view. Massive shoulders. Thickly muscled arms. Dark hair that fell in waves to his collar. Dark eyes that had mysteries locked in their depths. Okay, maybe Logan's scrambled brain was wishing on that last part. Pieces of memory wiggled on the periphery. Somehow he knew this man was safe.

He peered down at Logan, concern wrinkling his brow and chin. "My name is Tanzil Jareth. I'm a Warden. You're at my house. I rescued you."

"I can't move." Logan wiggled again, but his arms went nowhere.

"Here." Tanzil loosened the blankets. "I wrapped you up to keep you warm. The power's out. There's a violent storm outside that isn't letting up, and I didn't want to take the chance you'd kick off your covers while you were asleep."

Logan moved his arms. The right one screamed with pain. In fact, agony seared most of his right side. He moved the blankets and looked down. White bandages and gauze wrappings covered the affected areas, and something stank. "I got shot."

"Bullet grazed your right side. It's infected."

"What's that smell?" Logan nearly bit his tongue to keep that question inside. He didn't need to draw this sexy drink of water's attention to his odor problem. Considering where he'd been, he was surprised he didn't smell worse.

Another bit of memory returned. Logan recalled meeting conservation officer Tanzil Jareth before setting off on his adventure.

He'd found the game warden sexy, but he'd shooed away the thought because he'd been intent on clearing his head. Now that same dreamy warden had rescued him.

He pulled the blanket closer to keep the smell from escaping. "Nevermind."

Tanzil chuckled. "It's a poultice. I don't have antibiotics, which you need, and you have a fever. My Pawpaw taught me this kind of medicine. It's the best I can do right now." He glanced away, and then he sighed.

Logan followed his gaze, and realized the other man was looking out a large picture window. Though there was an overhang for the porch, wind drove the rain sideways, and it pounded against the glass. "Has it been raining like that since last night?"

Tanzil blinked away a twinge of surprise before his gaze returned to Logan. "It's been raining like this for two days."

"Two days?"

"You've been mostly unconscious. I've been waking you up every few hours to try to get you to eat or see if you can use the bathroom. I haven't been able to get anyone on the radio since the storm started, so I'm not sure if I'm doing anything right with regard to your care. At least you seem to be improving."

Tanzil was an alpha through and through, though Logan had never met an alpha whose idea of a good time included taking care of an invalid. He found this development counterintuitive.

Even with two days of rest, Logan was still tired. He closed his eyes and groaned. "I'm sorry for being such a pain."

"A pain? No—don't think that. I'm thankful I was able to save you. Doctors and nurses would know how to take better care of you. That's all I meant." He gestured to Logan. "Do you want to sit up? I'm heating up some soup. It's from a can, but it's all I can make over the fire right now."

A wave of nausea rolled over Logan. "I'm hungry, but I'm not sure I can eat."

"We'll start with water, sips of broth. This part, I know how to do from watching survivalist shows." A flash of excitement lit Tanzil's dark eyes. He lifted Logan's top half and shoved half a dozen pillows behind him. "There. How does it feel?"

Logan expected his side would ache more, but his pain level remained unchanged. He'd never felt so weak in his entire life. He didn't even think to protest when Tanzil cooled spoonfuls of broth by blowing on them before he fed each bite to Logan.

After a few bites, Logan's eyes grew heavy. Tanzil removed the pillows propping him up and tucked the blanket firmly around his shoulders. "Sleep is the best medicine right now. I think."

They continued like this for the rest of the day, with Logan eating a few bites before falling back to sleep, and by evening, Logan was able to stay awake for several hours. He even fed himself a small bowl of chicken noodle soup.

"How did you even think to look for me?"

Lounging on a ratty old recliner that seemed to swallow his large body, Tanzil stared into the fire. "It's my job. I'm a game warden. Conservation officer. Warden."

Something in the way Tanzil repeated 'warden' caught Logan's attention, but before he could ask, Tanzil continued.

"I went back to check in with you, and you weren't there, so I tracked you. I followed your scent until it disappeared."

Logan knew where his scent left off. "The edge of a clearing where rocks got bigger and bigger until they melted into the mountainside?"

Tanzil's gaze tore from the crackling flames. "It's a beautiful spot, but it's outside the wards that protect us."

Logan knew what the wards were. All bears knew to stay inside. "I didn't think you could just walk outside the wards without feeling it."

"That magic isn't meant to keep us in; it's meant to keep humans out. We're not prisoners."

Logan thought about that for a minute. "It's like putting up a private property sign."

"Pretty much, only the wards are more subtle, which makes them more effective. People aren't choosing to respect a sign. They're subconsciously being turned away at the borders."

"There should be warning signs posted so bears know that if they leave an area, their life may be in peril."

"Yeah." Tanzil said quietly. "Thousands of miles of borders. It's maybe better if a bear pays attention to boundaries. We used natural barriers like rocks, rivers, and cliffs to determine the borders. And, if you take time to look for the barriers, you should be able to sense them."

"Or that." Logan's gaze dropped. He'd grown up studying those maps, and he'd neglected to pay attention to the lessons his teachers had so patiently presented. What happened to him had been his fault. "I was not a good student."

Tanzil fell silent.

Having been alone for so long, Logan wanted to hear the sound of someone else's voice, and Tanzil had a very pleasant one. "So, after that, how did you find me?"

"Old-fashioned detective work." From Tanzil's sigh, Logan figured there was more to it than that.

"I don't know what that means," Logan prompted. "You canvassed the area looking for clues?"

"There was a sighting of a red SUV with a trailer leaving the area. I called down to Bear's Cove and had them run the plates. They gave me three addresses, and I visited them all." Tanzil's voice roughened, and Logan realized the process hadn't been as easy or unemotional as he tried to make it sound.

Logan's heart warmed, and he smiled. "You found me at the last one?"

"No. You weren't at any of them. I had Deputy Freeman do more digging while I visited Chad McConnell in the hospital—good work on taking him out, by the way—and he found an address for his brother, Jared."

Mentioning Dak Freeman sobered Logan. "Dak knows I'm missing? Does he know you found me?" He didn't want Chase to worry needlessly, not in his condition.

"He does. I was halfway to Bear's Cove when he called on the radio to warn me about the washouts and the bridge collapse."

Logan exhaled his relief. "Good. Not about the washouts and the bridge, but good that Dak knows I'm okay. That way Chase won't worry about me."

Tanzil nodded. "He said you were his husband's best friend."

"Yeah. Chase and I go back as far as I can remember."

They fell into silence again. The awkwardness grated on Logan's nerves. "Have I thanked you for saving my life yet?"

"Yeah. You're welcome."

That silence again. This time, Tanzil broke it. "Rain's letting up."

Logan peered out the window. Instead of only seeing to the railing of the porch, he could make out a waterlogged front yard, the lawn manicured right up until it met up with the trees that delineated the forest. "Is that a garden?"

"Yeah. It's late in the season, though, so everything's been harvested, except the pumpkins. I'm not sure they'll have survived this storm."

"Pumpkins are hearty. They have those thick shells."

Tanzil got up and went to the window. He stood with his hands behind his back, as if he could see the pumpkins from there. "They mildew quite easily. It's hit-or-miss with squash and me."

Logan had never tried to grow anything in his life. He had nothing to offer. There was a melancholy in Tanzil that Logan wanted to soothe away. Some kind of magnetism made him want to put his arms around Tanzil. That thought led to the next one—what Tanzil's lips might feel like against his own.

Then he shook away the inappropriate urge. Tanzil was older, a lot older, and he'd been nothing but kind to Logan. While Logan might be feeling attracted to the handsome, mature bear, he could discern no sign that Tanzil felt similarly.

The next morning, bright sunlight streamed through that great picture window. Logan turned on his right side to face away from it, but that only aggravated his injuries. Though it didn't hurt as much as it had the day before, he still groaned.

For the first time in far longer than he cared to remember, he rose on his own steam and completed his bathroom ritual alone. It might be a small victory, but to him it seemed momentous. Leaning heavily on the wall for support, he emerged from the bathroom.

Tanzil waited in the hall, his arms crossed over his bare chest. He looked Logan up and down, his dark chocolate eyes assessing the situation. "You're healing faster than I thought you would, considering you're not in a hospital."

Corded muscle defined the expanse of Tanzil's broad chest. The sight of those strong shoulders, thick biceps, and washboard abs caused Logan to salivate. He allowed himself the luxury of noting the way his flannel pajama pants stretched over his hips and thighs, accenting the power of the man who'd saved his life. Logan's fingers itched to reach out and see if that caramel skin was as smooth and silky as it appeared.

But he thought it might not be advisable to feel up someone who hadn't once looked at him as if he were a scrumptious meal. Logan cleared his throat and smiled. "You must have a magic touch."

Tanzil glanced away. "I'll make breakfast, and then I have to head out."

Logan's heart fell, surprising him because he hadn't realized how much he'd been looking forward to spending some time with the mysterious and remote man who'd rescued him and nursed him back to health. "Yeah. I guess you're anxious to get me back to Bear's Cove."

A frown furrowed Tanzil's brows. "It'll take a few days for the flood waters to crest and recede. You've healed enough to not need to be airlifted out of here, so we're going to have to wait for roads to reopen and the bridge to be repaired."

"Oh." None of this had occurred to Logan.

"Sorry, young one, but you're stuck here for at least another week, possibly two." Tanzil dropped his arms to his sides and padded toward the kitchen. "I'll see if I can raise anyone on the radio so I can report your progress."

Logan followed Tanzil down the hall and into the kitchen. It had a large, square shape with a lot of wood and surprisingly modern fixtures. Tanzil went to the far wall and slid back a panel, revealing a wall of radio equipment and a very large, flat-screen television.

"Wow," Logan said. "That's so cool. I never would have guessed those panels moved."

"My husband was a carpenter." Tanzil's voice suddenly seemed rusty and unused. "He disliked clutter, so he built storage for my equipment."

A stone lodged in Logan's stomach at the roughness of Tanzil's voice. Given the fact that nobody else was here, Logan deduced something tragic had happened to his rescuer's husband. He wanted to do something thoughtful like put a comforting hand on Tanzil's shoulder and offer his condolences, but the idea of the action seemed awkward and intrusive. Logan settled for something safe and utterly lame. "Well, he did a great job at concealing it."

He ran a hand over the smooth wood where the front panel disappeared behind the one next to it, and he envied Tanzil's husband's craftsmanship. Logan had no special talents. He'd proven mediocre at everything.

Tanzil's gaze flickered to where Logan touched the wood, and then he turned his attention to the radio. He flipped switches and turned dials, and then he picked up the microphone. "Warden Jareth here. Is anyone out there?"

While Tanzil adjusted settings and tried again, Logan limped to the other side of the kitchen. Though his legs were fine, he was weak and his hip hurt where the bullet had grazed the skin. He searched the cupboards for food, and he found a ton of canned soup. It looked like Warden wasn't much for culinary variety.

He opened the refrigerator, and a sour smell came out. Since Tanzil had been able to get his generator running, the refrigerator had remained cold, the toilet could flush, and the heat had run—albeit low. Tanzil had supplemented by keeping a fire blazing in the fireplace. Under very different circumstances, it could have been a romantic setting.

Tracing the sourness led him to expired milk, which he poured down the sink. There went his idea to make pancakes.

"Communications are still down." Tanzil came up behind him. "What are you doing?"

"Looking for something to scrounge up for breakfast. I was going to make pancakes, but your milk expired a week ago." Logan opened another cupboard, this one full of staples like peanut butter and more canned food. "When you said you had canned soup, I didn't realize it was your main source of food."

"I'm not much of a cook. I tend to grab whatever's handy."

Logan laughed. "Spoken like an alpha bear."

"There's meat in my deep freezer. I just don't like opening it up when the power is out. My generator is old, and I don't care to tempt fate where it's concerned." Tanzil opened another cupboard, one Logan hadn't yet checked out. "I have granola. I usually mix it up with some nuts and dried berries to make trail mix."

"For breakfast?"

Tanzil shrugged as he poured those ingredients into a cup. "You can eat whatever you want, young one. Make yourself at home."

Logan made coffee, and he ate the trail mix.

"So, where exactly are we?"

"About fifty miles northwest of Forrest Hills, half mile from the perimeter of the Warded Lands." Tanzil sipped his coffee. Steam rose from the mug, sending the pleasant aroma through the room.

That put him a good six hours or more away from Bear's Cove. Logan had never been so far from home. "What made you want to live way out here?"

"I'm a Warden. It's my job to protect and reinforce the Wards. I can't do that from deep in the interior." He shoved a handful of granola into his mouth. A dry piece stuck to his lip, and Logan wanted to brush it away.

Scratch that—he wanted to lick it away. Before he could stop himself, he reached out. His fingertip grazed Tanzil's full lower lip. A spark of electricity, a recognition so primal it didn't have a name, ran through Logan's body. He drew his hand back, acutely aware that Tanzil had gone still.

Chapter 5—Tanzil

Nerve endings Tanzil thought had gone dormant years before tingled and misfired, and he still felt the light caress of Logan's finger on his lip, lingering and urging him to act on the ancient need surging through his veins. His alpha nature, always simmering just below the surface, roared to life.

He shouldn't be having urges—even thoughts—like this about a bear who was at least a dozen years younger. Logan had been through hell, and the last thing he needed was for the man who'd rescued him to do the things Tanzil wanted to do.

Yet from the moment he'd first stumbled upon the sexy blond with the startling, sky-blue eyes, Tanzil had battled thoughts about what it would be like to kiss those luscious lips. And more—he wanted to peel away the baggy, borrowed clothes so he could explore every inch of Logan's body. Even starvation and torture hadn't been enough to alter his incredible allure.

Tanzil mentally shook himself and embraced all kinds of guilt. Not only did Logan need him to provide a sanctuary for his physical and emotional well-being, Tanzil had no business thinking about another bear that way. Namir had been gone for six years, but he was in every inch of the house. Even the mug from which Logan drank coffee had been chosen by Namir.

Rather than address anything that he was feeling, Tanzil got to his feet. "I'll be in and out most of the day, I think. I need to check on people, make sure they're okay, and see what roads are open and which aren't. Make yourself at home. I'll check back here in a few hours."

Without waiting for a reply, Tanzil left the kitchen. He snagged his jacket and headed for his truck.

Three hours passed quickly, and he made a point to run to the general store in the tiny village of Ursa Minor to pick up foods that Logan might like. Namir used to plan out meals and give Tanzil a list. Going from memory, he picked up yams, chickpeas, potatoes, fruit, bread, milk, and pancake mix. Hopefully something there would appeal to Logan.

He arrived home to find Logan crouching in the garden, his lanky frame covered with a dark jacket. Alighting from his truck, he called across the yard. "What are you doing?"

"Drying off your pumpkins so they don't mildew." He glanced up, a huge grin splitting his face. "They look good, Warden."

Mildew was in the soil. Drying them off wouldn't help, but he didn't want to burst Logan's bubble. Plus, Tanzil had never tried drying them off before, and since all his methods had failed, he was not an authority on gourds. He crossed the yard, his boots squishing in the waterlogged grass.

After the storm, the air had warmed considerably, though it was still in the high fifties. Logan wore a dark blue jacket over the baggy shirt and slacks that belonged to Tanzil. As he approached, Tanzil realized the jacket on Logan had belonged to Namir. Though he'd cleaned out most of Namir's things, donating them to various causes, every now and again he stumbled upon something he'd missed.

He'd missed the jacket. Namir had worn it on countless walks over the years. Seeing it on Logan, guilt blindsided him. He'd admired another man wearing Namir's clothes.

Logan rose, and his smile faded. "Tanzil? What's wrong?"

Shaking away his roiling emotions, he attempted to smile, but the gesture fell short. "Nothing's wrong. I bought groceries. I didn't know what you'd like, so I stuck to the basics."

Wiping his hands on his pants, Logan came out through the gate. Tanzil had fenced off the plot years before to keep out rabbits and deer. "I'll help you bring them in."

Tanzil put a restraining hand on Logan's arm. Unlike that morning, he didn't touch his skin. However that didn't seem to matter to his inner bear. The thing growled and clawed inside him, seeking to stake a claim. He forced the need into submission. "You should be resting."

Logan peered at him with wide eyes, the smaller bear tilting his face to meet his gaze. "I've been asleep for most of three days. I'm tired of sleeping."

"Young one, you need to rest or else you'll relapse."

Logan opened the gate of the fence and emerged from the garden. "I'm fine."

"I aim to keep you that way." Tanzil put his hand on Logan's lower back, guiding the younger man toward the house. The contact kept his bear in growling distance, but he couldn't seem to resist the need. "I have some of your clothes in my truck as well. I took them out of your truck so I could track you."

Inside, Logan shrugged out of the jacket and hung it in the front closet. Tanzil watched his actions, part of him wanting to be near in case Logan should need him and the rest of him wondering how he'd overlooked that jacket for so many years.

Logan rested his hands on his slim hips. "What's wrong?"

Tanzil started for the door. "I'll get the groceries."

Before he reached the entrance, Logan stepped in front of him. "Are you upset about the jacket? I was careful not to get mud on it."

Damn, but the younger bear was too perceptive by half. Tanzil dragged a hand through his thick hair. "It's fine. I just—I forgot I had it. It belonged to my husband."

Something lit in the back of Logan's pale eyes. "What was his name?"

"Namir."

"How long ago did you lose him?"

"Six years." Tanzil didn't want to continue this conversation. He picked Logan up and set him out of the way, and then he went to his truck.

Inhaling the cooler air, he got his libido under control. Talking about Namir with Logan was strange and oddly therapeutic, and he couldn't quite pinpoint why.

He loaded his arms with bags of groceries, and he remembered to snag his shifter pack with Logan's clothes still inside. As he approached the front door, it opened. Logan stepped out onto the porch, holding the screen door, but he wisely didn't offer to help carry anything.

Silent feet padded after him, following him to the kitchen. Once he set down the bags, Logan helped unload. The sounds of cupboards opening and items sliding on wood were the only noises except for their breathing.

When they finished, Logan leaned against the counter. "You know, if I cross a line or something, you can always just tell me you don't want to talk about it."

Not used to having to explain his past to anyone, Tanzil stared out the window over the sink. "Namir and I were married for ten years. He was pregnant with twin cubs when humans took him, and by the time I tracked him down, it was too late."

There—he'd shared the pertinent details.

"Is this the first time you've had a man here since he passed?"

It was the first time he'd had anyone there. He'd cut himself off from everyone, not letting those few persistent people farther than the front porch.

He felt Logan's hand on his arm, the thick fabric of his work shirt no match for the heat of the younger man's touch. Feelings zinged through Tanzil—desire and possessiveness—originating at the point of contact.

Being a Warden meant he was more in touch with the primal pieces of his shifter nature than most other bears. Right now, his inner bear roared for Logan Fordline. Heat washed through his body, a flame that could only be assuaged by this omega.

"Omega, I am barely holding on right now. Please refrain from touching me, and it would be best if you left the room."

He expected Logan to perhaps be hurt or upset. Pouting would be welcome because that was a huge turn-off for Tanzil. He waited for Logan to flounce away, but he only moved closer, wrapping his arms around Tanzil's midsection and resting his cheek against the back of Tanzil's shoulder.

"You didn't leave me to suffer alone, and I won't leave you."

Tanzil snorted, chuffing a sharp warning. "Young one, it isn't my grief that threatens you right now; it's my alpha nature. My bear wants you, and it's difficult to fight it with you so near." His bear hadn't wanted anyone since Namir, and the force with which it strained against its bonds stole his breath.

Logan's arms drew away, and he stepped back, but not far enough to quell the rising havoc inside Tanzil.

"Farther," he growled. "Go into the living room."

"I can't make lunch from there," Logan returned. "How about you go into the living room? Or you could go take a cold shower. Or you could just kiss me."

It was too much, and Tanzil was out of practice reigning in his alpha nature. Whirling, he lifted Logan, holding the smaller man's body against his own as his lips sought sustenance. He closed his mouth over Logan's, demanding submission from this omega. Logan softened against him, his arms twining around Tanzil's neck as the omega's lips parted on a sigh.

Tanzil's alpha nature stood up on its hind legs and let loose with a mighty roar. He deepened the kiss, plunging his tongue deep to stake a claim. The taste of him was like nothing he'd experienced before—sweet and spicy, and somehow liquid. It filled his senses and traveled his veins. He felt it in every corner of his body.

His hands roamed Logan's back, exploring the hard planes before venturing lower to squeeze handfuls of each delightfully rounded cheek. Small, gruff moans issued from Logan, feeding Tanzil's frenzy. He wanted to rip away the fabric covering Logan's body and bury his cock deep inside the submissive man, but he knew he wouldn't be able to temper his violence.

So he broke away, a brutal severing of their connection that sent his bear into a rage. Before he could do something he'd regret, he snagged his shifter pack from the counter, threw it around his torso, and bolted out the back door. He shifted to his bear form mid-step, shredding his clothes.

He ran from his home, his refuge.

He ran from the unexplained feelings he couldn't control.

He ran from the man he'd left standing in his kitchen who did things to him no man had done since his heart had died that horrific night so many years before.

Mostly, he ran from himself.

Chapter 6—Logan

Logan gripped the counter, his breaths coming fast and heavy, as if he'd just sprinted a mile. The room swam in and out of focus. Logan knew he wasn't back to full strength, but that didn't explain some of his symptoms, like the stabbing pain in his chest or the liquid heat simmering through his bloodstream.

Never in his life had a kiss affected him like that.

When he'd challenged Tanzil to kiss him, he'd been acting on instinct and reacting to the few sparks that arced between them whenever they touched. He hadn't expected to feel as if the alpha had seared his brand onto Logan's heart.

As he gathered his scattered wits, he realized something momentous had happened. Given Tanzil's reaction, the alpha had felt it, too. He'd tried to prevent it, but Logan had goaded him into losing control.

Across the room, the radio squeaked to life. "Tanzil? Buddy, are you there?"

Logan willed his legs to work, and he made his way to the radio. He wasn't sure how to use it, so he went with his instinct. He picked up the microphone and pressed the button. "This is Logan Fordline. Tanzil is out right now."

"Logan? Oh, thank goodness. This is Sheriff Bearsmith. How are you doing?"

"I'm recovering. Tanzil saved my life."

"That's fantastic to hear. Your fathers are here. They'd like to speak with you."

Before Logan could reply, his dad's voice came through the speaker. "Logan, I'm so happy to hear your voice."

If he wasn't mistaken, Marlin was crying. "Dad, I'm okay. Really."

His father, Arlen, came on next. "We've been worried out of our minds, son. We're happy that you're safe and sound. When do you think you'll be able to come home?"

Logan didn't particularly want to return home. He'd come out here to find himself, to decide what path in life he wanted to forge, and he hadn't done that yet. Plus there was the whole matter of the rift between him and his fathers. They'd refused to accept his friendship with Chase Longfellow because Chase's mother had been human. Chase had been good enough to work as a mechanic at their garage, but he hadn't been good enough to be Logan's best friend.

And that was just the start. They wanted him to be a lawyer. They'd pressured him to go to law school, and he'd hated every second of it. Only recently, when Chase had drawn a line in the sand, had Logan finally started to question why he'd formatted his life to his fathers' specifications instead of filling it with things that mattered to him.

He cleared his throat. "I don't know, father. Some of the roads are flooded, and a bridge was washed out, so I'll have to wait for the repairs. Tanzil said it might take a week or two."

Sheriff Bearsmith got back on the radio. "You said the warden was out?"

"Yeah." With the memory of Tanzil's kiss seared into his brain, Logan scrambled to create an explanation. "He said he had to check on people in the area to make sure everyone was okay."

"He's not answering his radio." The sheriff's frown came over the airwaves, loud and clear. "That's not like him."

"It wasn't working on our end. This is the first of anything we've heard over the radio. When he gets back, I'll let him know the radio is working."

"Okay. We need to clear the line. I'll have your fathers back tomorrow around the same time to talk to you. Bearsmith out."

"Sounds great. Fordline out." Logan grinned at his easy use of radio speak. Then he made lunch.

A few hours later, he thought about starting dinner. Hopefully Tanzil wouldn't stay out too late. Logan was a passable cook, but his buddy Chase was amazing. He went over to the wall of radio equipment and pressed a button he hoped would call Bear's Cove.

Nothing happened, so he pressed more buttons, including the one that let him talk to the sheriff and his fathers earlier. "Sheriff? This is Logan. Come in, Sheriff."

The static got louder, and then a voice broke through. "Logan, this is Dak. Sheriff Bearsmith is out of the office right now. How are you doing? You scared the hell out of Chase and me."

Logan grimaced because he hated putting the people he cared about through that. "Sorry about that. I wandered past the protection of the wards. I guess I never believed they were a real thing before now."

"They're real." A note in Dak's voice told Logan that there were things in this world he knew nothing about. Bear customs passed down to him had their roots in the mysteries of the universe.

He changed the subject, inching it toward the reason for his call. "How is Chase? Did he have the cub yet?"

Dak chuckled. "Chase is doing well, though he's tired of being pregnant. We're expecting the cub to come any day now."

Logan sighed. He'd wanted to be there for his best friend. "I promised I'd be there for him, and I'm not going to be able to get back."

"You just worry about keeping yourself safe. That's the most important thing. The cub will be here when you return, as will Chase."

"Dak? Is there any way I can talk to Chase?"

Static shot through the radio, a deafening noise that sent dials screaming and twirling. Then it settled down. "I'll call him. Stand by. Freeman out."

"Fordline out." He wasn't sure he was supposed to say that, but it seemed like the right way to end the interaction.

While he waited, he explored the house. There was meat in a deep freezer somewhere, and he aimed to find it. A door under the stairs revealed another set that went down instead of up. He flipped on the light switch and followed those. Downstairs he found a finished basement. Paneled walls lined a hallway the opened into a large, comfortable sitting room that looked like it hadn't been used in years. A layer of dust coated everything, though it was all in good repair and had probably been cleaned a few months prior. Mostly it seemed abandoned, forgotten—though this extra space seemed too much for one person.

"This house is fucking huge," he mumbled. He hadn't been upstairs yet, but from what it looked like outside, the upstairs was nearly as large as the main floor, which was sizeable. A family of six could live there comfortably, and there would still be space for a guest room on the main floor and all this basement space.

Next to the sitting room, he found a utility room, and that's where the deep freezer was located. It was long and white, like the kind in criminal shows that inevitably held a dead body. He shivered. Without Tanzil, that could have been his fate.

Breathing away the sudden panic that made his heart race, Logan opened the lid of the freezer and surveyed the contents. Tanzil had labeled everything, so it was easy to identify venison, beef, and fish. "Salmon. My favorite."

Upstairs, he ran warm water into a pan and set the salmon in it to thaw.

The radio crackled to life. "Logan? Logan, this is Chase. Logan, are you there? What? This button?" Static filled the airwaves for a second before they silenced.

Logan chuckled at the image of his buddy learning to let go of the speaking button so he could hear Logan's response. Of course, half a day ago, Logan wouldn't have known what to do either. He'd picked it up from watching Tanzil earlier.

"Chase, this is Logan. How are you doing?"

"Holy shit, Logan. It's great to hear your voice. I've been so worried about you. When Dak told me how they found you—" Chase's voice cut out with a sob.

"I'm okay." He rushed to assure Chase the danger had passed. "I have a cool new scar, and I've lost a few pounds, but hopefully you can help me gain them back."

"I'll cook for you." Chase sniffled. "I'll make lasagna and cake. Or pie. I made the best lemon meringue pie the other day. And chocolate volcano cake. I'll make anything you want."

Logan wished he could put his arms around his friend to reassure him, but he was sure Dak was next to Chase, doing the honors. "That sounds great, but right now I need a recipe for something to do with salmon. Tanzil isn't much of a cook, and I'm tired of eating canned soup. I'm sure he is as well."

"I didn't know you cooked." Chase's laugh followed the observation.

Living on his own for the past few months, he'd been watching cooking shows, and now he felt comfortable in the kitchen. "Chase, this is serious. The way to a man's heart and all that, you know?"

Silence through a radio was loud. Seconds passed. Finally, Chase's voice came through again. "You like this guy?"

"A lot. He's amazing, Chase. I've never met anyone like him." If he thought about it, Logan knew very little about Tanzil. But a part of him he'd never known existed recognized something in Tanzil. If Logan wanted to, he could theorize about fate or destiny or something like that, but he didn't know if any of those things existed. He only knew that Tanzil's kiss had brought to life an indescribable piece of Logan's soul that now drove him to do things like prepare a meal for the man he wanted as his alpha.

"Okay, I'll give you my most romantic fish recipe, but only if you tell me every detail. What does he look like? Have you kissed him?" Before Logan could reply, Chase interrupted with a dramatic sigh. "Wait on all that, okay? Dak says anyone can listen to what we're saying."

At the very least, Logan knew Tanzil wasn't in his car, listening in. Tanzil, in his bear form, was in the woods, running away from the combustible kiss they'd shared. As the omega, it was Logan's job to tame the beast. "Okay. Details when I get back. Recipe for salmon now."

A few hours later, the salmon was ready. He kept it warming in the oven while he made a salad. Tanzil came through the back door that led into the kitchen while Logan finished chopping carrots and radishes for the salad. Based on his shopping habits, Logan figured that Tanzil had a thing for root vegetables.

Logan smiled as Tanzil came inside, and he held that smile even though he was surprised to see the alpha fully clothed. "Just in time. Dinner's ready."

Taking only one step into the room, Tanzil set a rectangular cloth bag on the counter near the door. "I've arranged for you to stay somewhere else."

He didn't want to stay anywhere else. Rather than panic, he recognized the statement as part of the alpha's attempt to reestablish control, and he took it as a positive sign. "I'm fine here. Sheriff Bearsmith called on the radio while you were away. I assured him I was fine, and I told him you were out checking on people and wildlife and things."

Tanzil stared, his dark eyes heavy with torment and need. Underneath it all was a stony resolve.

Logan sought to circumvent that decision. "Let's eat first. I made salmon. I hope you don't mind that I went into the deep freezer. You said to make myself at home." He pushed up the sleeves on his shirt that had fallen past his wrists. Though Logan was not a small man, Tanzil was larger and longer. He threw a patient smile in Tanzil's direction. "Go ahead and get washed up. Dinner will be on the table in five minutes."

Tanzil's resolve wavered.

"Go on. I know you're hungry, and I spent a lot of time preparing this meal." Fish and potatoes. Logan had cubed the potatoes and baked them in butter and rosemary. He'd also sprinkled rosemary on the salmon to tie the dishes together. He wasn't sure about the whole idea, but Chase had assured him it would work.

Logan set the table in the dining room, another area of the house that seemed neglected. He'd spent an hour dusting and polishing the furniture and cleaning the floors. The dining table was an exquisite piece, simple and elegant. He'd found a runner in a drawer in the matching sideboard, and that bit of burgundy lent a romantic air to the whole setup.

Tanzil appeared as Logan set the platter of salmon in the center. He surveyed the scene with more than a little alarm.

Logan set a hand on the alpha's shoulder. "It's just dinner."

Some of the panic faded, and Tanzil moved away from Logan's comforting gesture. "Don't touch me."

It was good to know he still affected Tanzil because the alpha definitely affected Logan. His bear whimpered and whined, begging for attention from Tanzil, and Logan struggled to keep those submissive noises from escaping. First he had to convince Tanzil not to send him away.

Tanzil sat at the head of the table. Logan went to serve him food, but Tanzil waved him away. "You stay at the other end of the table."

They ate in silence for the first half of the meal. Logan watched Tanzil, his submissive side in tune with every move the alpha made.

Banking on the solid foundation he'd made through delicious food, Logan smiled across the table. "Do you like it? I haven't made salmon in a long time." He should credit Chase for giving him the recipe, but he didn't want to take the spotlight off himself. Chase would understand.

Tanzil barely paused. "It's very good."

"And the potatoes? I didn't know if you liked rosemary. They'll kind of suck if you don't like rosemary."

This time, Tanzil slowed down. "Logan, please understand I'm doing this to protect you. I didn't rescue you from humans and spend two days nursing you back to health just to be mistreated by me."

Logan poked at his potatoes. They glistened with butter, tempting his palate, but Tanzil's assurance bothered him too much to continue eating. "Define 'mistreated.'"

Tanzil's growl rumbled from the other side of the room. "Let it go, young one. When the flood waters recede, you'll return to Bear's Cove where you'll never again have to think about the borderlands."

Once upon a time, Logan would have shrugged at the rejection and walked away, but there was more riding on this interaction. He felt it in his heart and in a latent instinct he'd never before used. "You didn't answer my question."

This time the growl ripped from the alpha, rattling the plates on the table. "I'm a Warden, young one. I'm no one to trifle with."

"I have a great recipe for trifle, but I'll need fresh strawberries." Logan flashed a grin, letting Tanzil know that he wasn't afraid of him.

Tanzil's fists flexed next to his nearly empty plate. "You try my patience at your peril."

"Peril is overrated." It wasn't. Logan stiffened when he heard certain sounds, and he was certain the nightmares had just begun. However he didn't see that Tanzil could ever be a danger to him. Even

53

if he shifted and attacked him, Logan would shift and submit. In that way, his bear form was much simpler than his human form.

"I see from your reckless claim you have no idea what a Warden is."

"Conservation officer. You make sure everyone treats the environment and natural resources with respect and care. You give tickets to people fishing or hunting without a license. You stock ponds when they get low on fish, and you take wounded animals to shelters. I know what a game warden does." Logan sipped water and resumed eating. "I understand that your job can be dangerous, but I don't see how it makes you dangerous."

"I'm a Warden, young one. I cast, protect, and reinforce the wards that keep humans out. Being a conservation officer pays the bills and allows me to fulfill my oath to keep shifters safe from human interference." He leaned closer the tiniest bit. "As a Warden, I'm more in touch with my wild side."

Logan stared for the longest time, fitting together what he knew with pieces of lore he'd heard. He recognized that Tanzil was a *Warden*, not just a warden. "Is that how you found me—with magic?"

"It's not magic, though I suppose if you don't understand the mystical nature of shifters, it could seem that way." He exhaled hard. "I tracked you the old-fashioned way, though my senses are more developed because I'm a Warden. Once the trail went cold, I called on the mists to show me what had happened. I didn't get much, only a red SUV with a trailer attached."

"That's where your day job comes in handy. You called the sheriff for addresses of cars matching that description." Logan put his hand over his heart. "Thank you for not giving up, Tanzil. I owe you my life."

The alpha shook his head, an ominous expression darkening his face. "You don't owe me anything, least of all your life. That's why I have arranged for you to stay elsewhere. My bear wants you, and it will not take you gently."

Logan ran his hand along the edge of the table as he thought. Tanzil had been married for ten years, which meant he was capable of having sex without harming his partner. "I like rough sex. I only ask that you use lube. You didn't buy any, but olive oil can work just as well, though it will probably stain your sheets."

Tanzil gripped the arms of his chair, and his eyes glittered like obsidian. "There is no way to stop me once I start, young one, and that's all in addition to my kinky side."

"Bondage?" Logan's cock stood up and cheered. "Yes, Warden. Yes to all of it."

Tanzil pushed his chair away from the table and stalked from the room.

Before the alpha could shift and run away, Logan hurried after him, but Tanzil was headed toward the stairs. He slid in front of Tanzil, perching one hand on the banister and the other on the wall to block the way. "Warden, I'm a consenting adult."

"You're a misguided cub with no sense of self-preservation."

He lifted his shirt overhead, and then he let the large garment fall to the floor. The scar on his side didn't diminish all the work he'd done to sculpt his body to perfection. Perhaps he was a bit on the thin side now, but that would change with a few good meals. "I'm an omega whose bear is begging and pleading for your touch."

Then he stopped suppressing the primal urges his bear felt. An ursine whine sounded deep in his throat, the unique call of an omega begging for his alpha's dominance.

Tanzil closed his eyes. "Fuck, Logan. I don't want to hurt you."

"What makes you think I won't like it?"

His eyes flew open, raw desire reflected in those chocolate depths. "If you fight me, I will quell you. I'm talking bear teeth and claws."

Though he desperately wanted to touch Tanzil, Logan knew better than to move. "And if I behave, can I come in your mouth?"

The alpha's gaze turned predatory, but he said nothing.

"Please, Warden?"

Tanzil's mouth crashed into his as the captured Logan with a kiss. This one was different from before. While it was just as dominating, it established an irrefutable claim that Logan was powerless to resist.

Logan slid his hands up Tanzil's arms to grip his strong shoulders as he moaned into the onslaught. Liquid heat raced through his synapses, firing random signals to the pleasure centers in his brain.

Effortlessly, Tanzil lifted him. Logan helped by wrapping his long legs around his alpha's waist. He hadn't been upstairs yet, almost as if he'd been waiting for this kind of invitation. Tanzil's kiss went on and on, stealing his breath in a way that made him never want to breathe again.

This time when Tanzil broke the kiss, it lacked violence, but it was full of promise. He set Logan down, sliding the omega down his body. With the pull of a string, he released the tie holding the borrowed sweats around Logan's waist. They fell to his ankles, baring his body and revealing evidence of his desire.

Tanzil stepped back, his gaze moving in a slow caress over Logan's exposed flesh. Though acutely aware he was the object of Tanzil's attention, Logan noted basic information about the room.

A large bed with four, blocky posts dominated the room. On the interior wall was a matching dresser. The posts sticking up from the back of the dresser supported a large mirror. The outside wall featured large windows with two overstuffed chairs arranged invitingly under them. Two doors broke the monotony of the cream-colored wall opposite the bed. Through the open one, Logan spied a shower, the curtain open to reveal taupe tile.

The covers on the bed—a burgundy comforter and matching sheet—were a mess, tangled and tossed aside.

Logan stood halfway between the dresser and the bed, the door to the hall open to remind him that he had a way out.

He didn't want a way out.

Tanzil moved around him, touching him with only the power of his gaze, but it packed physical force. Every nerve ending in his body came alive. He didn't move an inch.

He felt Tanzil's breath on his neck and the tickle of his fingertips as they brushed against his hips. On his right side, the caress grazed the bandage that covered his wound, momentarily arresting Tanzil's intent.

"Young one, I will try to remember your injury."

His voice held too much gravity. Logan sought to ease the tension, so he laughed. "Well, Warden, at least we both know you can make one hell of a poultice."

Tanzil's lips pressed against the side of his neck, nesting in the curve where it met his shoulder. He stayed like that for a moment, and then he banded his arms around Logan, pinning his arms to his sides. His mouth opened.

Logan shivered in anticipation. Sharp points punctured his flesh, sending flashes of unexpected pain through him. He cried out, but he didn't fight Tanzil's hold. When Tanzil had talked about biting, Logan had pictured an erotic bite, the kind that made his dick hard. Biting like this wasn't common among bears, and for the first time, he realized that Tanzil's warnings had been honest and heartfelt.

This bite skewered him, canine teeth penetrating first before the rest of the teeth sank in.

Tanzil didn't seek to quiet his shout. Logan silenced himself, breathing through the fiery agony. Slowly it faded, and languor spread from the point of contact. He felt himself submitting to this alpha in a way he'd only pretended before now.

The hold around Logan eased, and Tanzil's hands roamed Logan's chest. One came up to circle his throat, the light pressure more possessive than threatening. Tanzil extracted his teeth from Logan's flesh, and the hand at his throat moved to cup his face, turning it until Tanzil's lips slanted over his.

While he plunged his tongue into Logan's mouth, his hand closed around Logan's cock, lazily pumping up and down the length. Logan moaned, and Tanzil swallowed the sound, claiming it as he did every inch of Logan's body.

He didn't know how long the kiss lasted, but by the time Tanzil released him, Logan's chest heaved, seeking oxygen.

"Clothes," Logan panted. "You're wearing too many. Let me strip search you, Warden."

A laugh rumbled from Tanzil's chest and into Logan's back. "All in due time, omega." As he talked, Tanzil's fist kept up a steady rhythm.

Pleasure built swiftly. Logan rested his head back on Tanzil's shoulder. "That feels so good. I'm close."

Tanzil's ministrations ceased. "You don't get to come yet." He dropped a kiss on Logan's forehead. "Get on your knees, facing me."

Logan knelt on the thin rug, the rough grain digging into his knees.

"Clasp your hands behind your back. Widen your knees." He watched as Logan complied, and then he flashed a brief smile. "Excellent."

Tanzil unbuttoned his brown, conservation officer shirt, revealing a smooth expanse of cinnamon skin that gave Logan ideas about licking and biting. Once it was unbuttoned, he opened it up. Muscles, large and corded, rippled under that kissable skin. He let his gaze roam, drinking in the gorgeous sight he wanted to touch so badly.

When Tanzil undid his fly, Logan licked his lips. Once the pants and underwear were gone, Logan sighed in anticipation. Tanzil's erect cock, nestled in a tangle of curls, was darker than the rest of his skin, and his large sack swayed underneath, inviting some of that licking and biting.

Taking his cock in hand, Tanzil masturbated, teasing Logan with the proximity.

"Please," he whimpered. "Let me touch you."

"Warden."

The order redirected his attention. "What?"

"Call me Warden. I like it."

Logan moistened his lips and let saliva pool in his mouth. "Warden, please let me suck your cock."

Tanzil stroked his cock a few more times, and then he tapped the tip against Logan's bottom lip. "Open. Get it wet."

He opened his mouth, and Tanzil slipped the tip inside, slowly working it deeper as Logan's mouth produced saliva as lubricant. Once he was slick enough, he withdrew almost completely. "Relax your jaw, and when it feels like you're going to choke, swallow."

Logan had given his fair share of blowjobs before, but he'd always used his hands. With Tanzil, he knew he wouldn't be given that courtesy. Tanzil surged forward, burying his cock to the hilt. Logan swallowed convulsively, but that didn't ease the choking sensation. His face reddened, and his muscles tensed with the effort. His eyes watered. Tanzil didn't move his cock, but he did caress Logan's brow.

"You're so fucking gorgeous, omega. That mouth is hot and luscious, and the tears making your eyes glassy only makes me want to fuck you harder." With that, he withdrew, and Logan frantically inhaled through his nose before Tanzil could push to the back of his throat again.

Tanzil set a furious pace. Nothing about it was gentle. He crushed Logan's lips against his teeth with each thrust, letting him know he had lost control. Moans tore from Tanzil, and that evidence of pleasure made pride swell in Logan's chest. He whimpered in submission, the vibrations stroking his alphas cock.

All too soon, Tanzil withdrew. He hadn't orgasmed in Logan's mouth, and the omega felt a sense of loss.

But not for too long. Tanzil lifted him, and their lips met. His hungry mouth devoured Logan's, and Logan submitted to the act. He pressed his chest to Tanzil's, luxuriating in the silky feel of Tanzil's skin against his and the way the alpha's hands roamed Logan's sensitive flesh. Logan caressed Tanzil everywhere he could reach—chest, arms, shoulders, back—and when he cupped Tanzil's face in his hands, the alpha's frenzy eased.

He lifted Logan, carried him three steps, and set him on the bed. Then he bent down to continue the kisses, and his hand stroked Logan's cock.

Tanzil ended the kiss. "Scoot back, omega, and lay on your stomach."

Logan obeyed.

"Arms above your head."

Logan stretched his arms up, across the huge bed. Tanzil wrapped thick leather bands around Logan's wrists and buckled them in place. Then he attached them together. Logan grinned at this light bondage. "Oh, Warden, I can handle more than this."

"I'm sure you can, omega, and that will come later." Tanzil's smile had a bit of a chill to it. "Open your mouth."

Thinking he was going to get another taste of that delicious cock, Logan opened wide, but he found the ball of a gag being shoved past his lips. Before he could protest, the thing was secured into place.

There were no neighbors to protest the noise, so this was purely for Tanzil's titillation. Logan peered at his alpha, his steady gaze hopefully communicating trust and desire.

Tanzil stroked Logan's head, reminding him that his blond locks were a thing of the past. He didn't mind the shorter hair so much, not with the way it let him feel Tanzil's caress. Leaning down, Tanzil sucked Logan's earlobe into his mouth. Then he bit it without breaking the skin. Logan had yet to look down to see what Tanzil had done to his shoulder. Though it throbbed to the same beat as his cock, it no longer hurt.

Then Tanzil climbed onto the bed and settled his weight on Logan's back. "I'm going to fuck you, omega. The gag is because I enjoy the way it looks in your mouth. Feel free to get as loud as you can."

His fingers probed Logan's tight hole, spreading lube around the entrance. Then he felt the wide head of Tanzil's cock breach that tight hole, and he exhaled to welcome his alpha inside. Tanzil thrust all the way home. Logan cried out, more from surprise than anything else. Tanzil's cock filled him, and pleasure thrummed through his blood.

Tanzil stroked a caress down Logan's arm. "This is where I get rough, omega. Brace yourself."

With that, he withdrew until the head of his cock again stretched Logan's entrance. For a second time, he thrust all the way inside, reaming Logan again. The sensation stole his breath, but Tanzil didn't wait for him to acclimate.

Over and over, Tanzil reamed him. The thrusts came faster and harder. It hurt and it felt good. Shards of pleasure pricked all over Logan's body, and his mind took flight. He fought Tanzil, not to dislodge him or make him stop, but because he'd gone to a primal place that screamed for more and faster.

Claws pressed into his back, holding his torso down as Tanzil pounded into his ass. His alpha's breaths came faster and faster. Logan's cock rubbed against the sheet, a sweet torment that urged the start of a climax to bloom in his balls.

Suddenly that paw came around front, and a hand encircled his throat. The claws, still there, grazed his neck and shoulder, warning him not to fight the inevitable. It was hot, erotic and dominant, utterly Tanzil, and it touched something deep inside Logan. He cried out, and he came before Tanzil's guttural cry accompanied the hot jets of seed that marked his climax.

The alpha bear collapsed on top of Logan, and the claws retracted, morphing back into a hand. The band holding the ball gag in place slackened, and Tanzil turned them so that his larger body wrapped around Logan's smaller one. His fingertips stroked a soothing rhythm down Logan's arm.

Stunned by the intensity of the sex and of his orgasm, Logan trembled in Tanzil's arms. He'd never felt so connected to another shifter in his entire life.

"I'm okay," he assured the alpha. "I promise, Warden—you weren't too rough."

Tanzil's breath quickened. "I'm not finished, omega. That was merely the warm-up."

Logan surveyed the cuffs on his still-bound wrists. "I like the bondage and stuff, but I'm afraid to look at my shoulder." The throbbing had eased, and the sting had disappeared, so perhaps the bite hadn't been as bad as he'd thought.

The alpha's hand moved up his arm and settled over the affected area. "Warden bites are rarely lethal."

"What?" Logan leaped from bed and examined his neck in the mirror over the dresser. Two small dots, already scabbed over, remained. "You were kidding."

Tanzil propped himself up on an elbow, an image of sex incarnate. He grinned. "I have a sense of humor."

"You were all doom-and-gloom with the violent sex predictions. That's not funny."

His smile faded. "Not funny, but serious. Logan, I fought my inner bear because I don't want to hurt you. That's why I began with a bite. I thought that if I marked you, it would placate my bear. Binding you and using the gag—it rendered you powerless, and that worked in your favor as well."

Logan returned to the bed. He crawled across the mattress, his movements awkward and slow due to the cuffs. "I think you're full of shit."

Tanzil's serious expression hardened. "Omega, you're walking a fine line here."

"Yeah, whatever. I think you just like the kinky stuff. That's not an enhanced bear side because of your Warden training. That's just your dominant side coming through. It's okay to like bondage. It's even okay to be a sadist, as long as you have your omega's consent for whatever kinky thing you want to do." Logan rolled his eyes as he knelt next to the alpha. "It's a whole lifestyle. It's nothing to be ashamed of."

"I'm aware that it's a lifestyle. I'm alpha and dominant. I was doing this when you were still a cub. Trust that I know the difference between what my bear wants and what's good for you."

Logan traced a line up Tanzil's inner thigh. "What does your bear want that you won't give it?"

Chapter 7

Tanzil

A mate. Tanzil's bear wanted a mate, but he knew that he couldn't be a husband and alpha to another omega. Losing Namir had shattered him, and he had nothing left to give to another person.

But he couldn't say that to Logan. The younger man wasn't fishing for a long-term relationship, which was why Tanzil had finally allowed himself to be seduced. Neither of them was doing more than seeking refuge in the aftermath of a storm.

In lieu of an answer, Tanzil seized Logan by the back of his neck and forced the omega to lean down for a kiss. He thrust his tongue past Logan's lips and staked a temporary claim. Logan moaned and returned the kiss, sliding his body closer to press it against Tanzil's. He clutched at Tanzil the best he could with his bound hands.

"Are you ready for more?"

"Yes, Warden.

He spent the rest of the night practicing restraint—literally and figuratively—and when soft cries of fright woke him, he took Logan in his arms and soothed the omega without waking him.

The next morning, he awoke to the scent of bacon sizzling. His nose led him down the stairs and to the kitchen. He found Logan in front of the stove, singing as he flipped pancakes. The sexy omega wore a pair of Tanzil's sleep pants with the cuffs of the legs rolled up.

Tanzil watched the domestic scene, allowing his inner bear this brief moment of contentment, until he noticed the emblem on Logan's shirt. Though the shirt was plain white, the orange emblem on the front with a saw and chisel was all too familiar. Blood left his extremities, and Tanzil felt cold all over.

Logan turned around, setting a platter on the counter behind him, and his face brightened. "Warden, you're up. I was going to surprise you with breakfast in bed." Then he frowned. "What's wrong?"

Shaking himself, he inhaled sharply. "Nothing. You wore me out last night."

Logan chuffed. "After a full night's sleep, you should be recharged. You're not *that* much older than me."

Twelve years was a long time. It meant generational differences and tons more life experience on Tanzil's part. He was of the age that wanted to settle down and have a family. Logan was still young and reckless, as the trouble he'd courted on the mountain proved.

Rather than respond, Tanzil went to the refrigerator and took out a carton of orange juice. When he closed the door, he found Logan waiting, arms crossed, on the other side.

"Out with it."

It looked like Logan had found his inner mother hen. Tanzil sighed. "That's Namir's shirt. I'd forgotten I had it."

Logan looked down, frowning at the shirt. "Sorry. I'll take it off."

Tanzil put a restraining hand on Logan's arm. His warm skin was silky and inviting. "No, don't. It's okay. Where did you find it?"

"Hanging in the closet. I grabbed a shirt without looking because I didn't want to disturb you." His gaze met Tanzil's. "I didn't mean to cross a line."

Tanzil bit his upper lip, sucking it into his mouth for a second. "You didn't cross a line. Your clothes are stranded with your truck, and Namir's stuff fits you better than mine." He ran a hand through his hair. "I don't have much around, but you're welcome to whatever you find."

If he'd been there, Namir would have been the first person passing out his clothes to Logan. Of course, if he'd been there, Tanzil wouldn't have spent the night burying his cock in Logan's body. Even now, his cock stirred, threatening to point in Logan's direction.

Logan kissed his cheek. "Thank you, Warden."

He used the name like a title, paying respect to his alpha. Tanzil couldn't stop the rising tide of desire coursing through his system. His bear wanted Logan, and now that he was available, it wouldn't be denied.

Before Logan could move away, he snatched him closer and laid an open-mouthed kiss on the omega. Immediately his lover softened, submitting to him. When he ended it, Logan said, "How about breakfast first? It's better if you eat it before it gets cold. Then we can do whatever you want, Warden."

"Fine. Let's eat in here." The kitchen featured a small table with four chairs. Over the past six years, Tanzil had routinely eaten in the kitchen. Until last night, he'd avoided the dining room with the furniture that Namir had so lovingly made. The table sat six because Namir had wanted at least four children. He'd fashioned a movable leaf in case they decided on more.

Tanzil shook away the ashes of those dreams. Logan was a distraction, a promise of hot sex, not a replacement for the man he'd loved. He poured juice for them both, and he brought napkins to the table.

Logan had already set out their plates and forks. He'd heaped pancakes and bacon onto each plate, and he'd put a bottle of syrup on the table. He tucked into the food with a voracious appetite. "Do you have to work today?"

"Yes." Tanzil cut into the stack of pancakes. "I'll likely be out most of the day." He'd neglected his duties the day before. When he'd left in bear form, he'd run for quite a distance. Then he'd shifted and he'd cited seven unlicensed off-road vehicles that had been out riding private trails without permission. Other than that, he hadn't done much.

"Okay. Is there anything I should do around here?"

Tanzil glanced around. He had no phone or access to internet, and the antenna to his television had been knocked down in the storm. The radio was his only means of contact. When Namir had been alive, he'd spent most of his time fixing up the house, working on his carpentry projects for his business, and being a househusband. "You can do whatever you want, I guess."

Logan dipped bacon in syrup. "Can I shift into bear form if I stay close to the house?"

"Sure. If you follow the path out the back gate, it leads alongside a creek that runs into a river that's great for swimming."

Logan's gaze turned introspective.

The urge to delve deeper, to find out his lover's thoughts, assailed Tanzil, but he pushed it aside. They'd been thrown together by circumstance, not choice, so he continued on the vein. "The boundaries for the wards aren't far from here, so be careful. I keep them reinforced pretty well. I haven't had a breech since I've taken over as Warden in these parts."

A bit of color left Logan's face. "How do I know if I'm at the edge of the wards or if I've gone past them?"

"Look for natural borders, like water or cliffs. Anytime you go from a covered area to an open area, be wary. If you stop and listen, you can hear a difference in the way things sound. On our side, it's crisper and more vibrant. On the other side, it's muted."

With his fork, Logan pushed around the last of his meal. "I thought that was just because I was freaked out, and they kept shocking me with this metal thing."

"Cattle prod."

Logan jerked as if he'd been hit with it again, and a hint of haunted wildness came into his eyes.

Tanzil reached across the small table, setting his hand over Logan's. "You're safe here. I won't let anything happen to you."

His gaze dropped, and his shoulders hunched as waves of melancholy emanated from him. "I came out here hoping something would happen to me."

Most people who brought camping gear meant to get away from the city for a relaxing weekend. Tanzil wondered if Logan referred to something more than time to get in touch with his inner bear. That need to delve returned, and he acquiesced. "Like what?"

A shoulder lifted and fell, but his gaze remained downcast. "Like— I don't know. I'm kind of at a crossroads in my life. I got a degree in political science because my fathers want me to go to law school, but I dislike working in an office, and I dread spending my days dealing with legal issues. Everyone I know has figured out what they want. My best friend, Chase, likes to fix things. He worked for my fathers as a mechanic for a while, and now he's opened an appliance repair company. Since we were kids, he's been passionate about fixing things. His eyes light up when he sees a broken toaster."

Tanzil chuckled. "I could have used him a month ago when my toaster caught fire."

The ghost of a smile curved Logan's lips, and then it was gone. "I've never had a passion for anything, and I'm useless when it comes to most things." His gaze roamed the kitchen, taking in the whole room. "You're passionate about being a Warden. Your husband was obviously passionate about carpentry. I've never seen such elegant woodwork, and it's through the whole house. Was he always into working with wood?"

Memories—good ones—rushed back, and Tanzil grinned. "He always had a project or an idea for one. When I met him, he was building a cabinet. I was in training as a conservation officer, and he'd called about finding an injured barred owl. When we got there, I found him etching an owl design into the front of the cabinet. The owl was safe in another cabinet, where he'd crawled after he got injured." He'd complimented Namir's work, and that was the beginning of their relationship.

"See what I mean? I'm almost twenty-four. I have a college degree, and I have no idea who I am or what I want." He shook his head. "I was hoping a few days in the woods would focus my mind and help me figure out why I'm here."

He fell silent, and Tanzil knew he was fixated on what had gone wrong. Letting him fall down that rabbit hole wasn't going to lead anywhere good, so Tanzil squeezed his hand, drawing him back to the present. "Not everyone settles on a career path in their twenties. I became a conservation officer because my father was one, and I thought that's what people in my family did when they grew up. It wasn't until I was thirty that I embarked on a path to becoming a Warden."

"But it's a natural step. It's where you were heading all along."

Sadness seized Tanzil. "I didn't head there until Namir was murdered. It was an act of grief and desperation. At the time, it seemed like the only thing I could do."

Logan gazed at him, a wealth of understanding blazing from those sky blue eyes. But there was a longing as well, and an anguish that wouldn't fade anytime soon.

There was nothing he could do except try to chase away the bad memories and replace them with something good. He stood, urging Logan to his feet, and he took the omega in his arms. "You're going to get through this," he promised. "Spend today doing what you originally intended. The river is the perfect place for introspection."

Tanzil had spent a lot of time there after losing Namir, and that was the place where he'd come to terms with living a solitary life.

As he drove around the protected lands, responding to calls, his mind was back at home with the tortured young man he regarded with affection. When he'd first met the omega, he'd found him attractive, but he'd dismissed the idea they might have anything in common. And perhaps they hadn't. Logan's life hadn't been touched by horror or tragedy.

Tanzil breathed through the pang of regret. He couldn't have predicted what happened to Logan, and he couldn't have prevented it from happening. He was a Warden. Though it afforded him certain powers, he couldn't divine the future.

He could only deal with the present.

At present, Logan Fordline needed him to help the healing process. If he could help Logan heal, it would be a bit of penance for not being able to save his family.

His radio crackled to life, so he pulled to the shoulder to respond. "This is Warden Jareth."

"Hey, Tanzil. Cord here. I have some news. Chad McConnell was released from the hospital today. Charges have not been filed against him or Emily McConnell."

Rage burned in his esophagus. "What the fuck? Why not?"

"They're maintaining they had a bear in the cage, not a person."

In an attempt to get his temper under control, he exhaled hard. "I submitted a preliminary report yesterday—with evidence."

"I saw it. They have pictures, geo-time stamped because they took them with their cell phone. It shows a bear."

Tanzil gnashed his teeth. He fucking hated humans. "We can't let them get away with this. Did they pick up Jared McConnell?" At the very least, they had him for torture and imprisonment of Emily McConnell.

"Emily McConnell declined to press charges. The local prosecutor doesn't see grounds for a case."

Before his temper hit a critical point, he went over the pieces of evidence in his head. If they wanted to go with unlawfully caging a bear, he could work with that. "I'll have to head back over there to recover more evidence."

"You need a warrant?"

"Follow-up. I'm a conservation officer. If they want to insist that they had a bear in there, then that's my purview. Cord?"

"Yeah?"

"They put a man in that cage and tortured the hell out of him. They put a woman in there as well. According to them, they locked her in there with a wild bear. Can you lean on the prosecutor? There's a case for something here. Those fuckers can't go free."

"I'm working on that. I wanted to keep you in the loop. Bear River crested today. Once it goes down, they'll be able to repair the bridge. How is Logan doing?"

"He's okay." He didn't want to reveal personal information, but he needed to. "He's eating well, but he still has nightmares."

"I can send a chopper to pick him up."

"No." The refusal was out of his mouth before he could think about why he didn't want Logan to leave. "He's out of medical danger."

"Okay, but if things change, call me. I'll have a MedEvac there in two hours."

"Got it. Jareth out."

He set the receiver back in its spot and stared at the trees lining the two-lane road winding through his domain. He should give Logan the choice to stay or go. If Cord was offering the MedEvac, that meant everyone with a medical emergency had been handled.

He put the vehicle in gear and continued to his next destination, a lake where someone had reported that a poacher was shooting at loons.

Logan

The path proved simple to find, beginning on the other side of the garden as Tanzil had described. It was well-worn, the foliage beaten down from regular use. He realized that this place must be special to Tanzil.

Having left his borrowed clothes back at the house, Logan shifted. His senses came alive, and he caught Tanzil's scent immediately. It washed through his being, triggering a feeling of contentment and peace.

Nose to the ground, he followed the trail until he came to the river. Once there, he explored the area the way a bear does—with his sense of smell. Tanzil was all over the place. His scent was on the grass near the bank and on the trees around the perimeter. He'd marked this place, claiming it as his own, and he had permitted access to Logan.

Surrounded by a feeling of security he'd never quite enjoyed before, he stretched out on the bank in a place where the grass was flattest and Tanzil's scent was the strongest.

Wrapped in peace, he let his senses go, opening them until he felt no difference between himself and the ground cradling his ursine form. Sounds of forest creatures created a symphony that carried his consciousness to the very barrier keeping bears safe. The Wards were a product of the same mysticism that made him a shifter. He felt the truth of that in his core. He'd never considered himself close to nature or part of something larger, but out here, he felt it.

Though he hadn't known what he'd wanted to find when he'd set out on this quest, he'd found it.

Thanks to Tanzil, the Warden with sorrow in his heart, he'd found a sense of belonging and contentment he'd never imagined possible.

Now he had to figure out what to do with it. That understanding eluded him.

When he returned to the house, the scent of venison and spices came from a crock pot sitting on the kitchen counter. The sweats he'd left on the counter next to the back door were gone.

"Warden? Are you home?" He hoped so. It would be awkward to stumble upon a stranger while walking naked through the house. Also, he doubted a stranger would make dinner.

"Upstairs." Tanzil's voice floated down from the bedroom.

With a grin, Logan mounted the steps. It looked like his alpha lover had come home early with naughty thoughts on his mind. He sailed into the bedroom, expecting to find Tanzil naked, or at least in the room. It was empty, and a gossamer curtain billowed as a breeze came through the room. "Where are you?"

A shadow passed in front of the window, and Tanzil stepped through the opening. "I was sitting on the roof over the garage." He closed the window, cutting off the cool, fall air. "I can see over the trees and find holes in the Wards."

"Did you find any?"

"No. They're holding strong." He turned around, and his gaze moved over Logan's body. A fire lit in his eyes.

"Someone moved the clothes I left in the kitchen." Logan grinned at Tanzil's open appreciation. "I guess I'm staying naked tonight."

Tanzil swallowed and glanced away. His hand fisted before he spread his palm on his thigh. "Cord said they can send a MedEvac for you if you need to get home now, before the river recedes and the roads open."

Hot and cold shards raced through his bloodstream and lodged in his throat. His heart beat so fast, it felt like it was going to explode. Logan's breath came faster. "You want me to leave?"

"I don't want to keep you here if you're anxious to get home. You're not a prisoner, Logan, and I know your family and your life are in Bear's Cove. You're free to go where you please. It's your call, not mine."

The panic melted away. Tanzil wasn't making him leave the sanctuary he'd found here. "If it's okay with you, I'll wait until the roads open."

Tanzil's gaze returned, as did his smile. "It's fine with me. Did you find the creek?"

"Yes. It's everything you said it would be." Even thinking about it made peace flow through him. "Thank you for sharing it with me. I'd like to spend more time there."

"Sure." He held Logan's gaze, a single line of sight was stronger than any bondage cuff. "Last night was good for both of us. I think you needed the connection to help heal your psyche, and perhaps I did as well."

Logan hadn't expected Tanzil to psychoanalyze what had happened. They'd acted on attraction and instinct. While he hadn't thought last night had cemented them into a serious relationship, he'd anticipated a few more blissful nights in his Warden's arms. "That sounds like a break-up line."

"It's not. I just meant I don't expect you to sleep with me while you're here. You mentioned that you undertook this quest to find yourself, and I want you to do that." He spread his arms, indicating the whole of the house. "I want this to be a safe space for you. I don't want you to feel obligated. You don't owe me anything."

Now he understood. Tanzil wasn't rejecting him. The alpha was reminding him that sex was a choice, and he had the option to say no.

He crossed the room, closing the distance, stopping inches from Tanzil's tense body. "That's fantastic, Warden, but I was hoping the unbelievable sex would continue." He drew a fingertip along Tanzil's strong jaw. "Unless you'd prefer I stay in the guest room?"

In lieu of an answer, Tanzil gripped the back of Logan's neck and ravaged his mouth. Flames ignited, and they both ripped at Tanzil's clothes. The Warden had changed out of his work uniform, but the flannel shirt he'd replaced it with had just as many buttons. Logan undid a few, and then he tugged it over Tanzil's head.

The alpha lifted him, and they came down on the bed. Rolling and wrestling, they stripped away Tanzil's pants. He pushed Logan onto his back and settled between his legs. He drizzled lubricant onto his cock, and then he spread Logan's legs wider. "You're so fucking sexy, omega. When you came in here, I wanted to throw you down and fuck you senseless instead of offering you a way out."

He lined the head of his cock up with Logan's hole and pressed forward. Logan felt the stretch, the delicious sting making his dick jerk in response, and then he felt full.

Whole.

Sex had never made him feel whole before. It was pleasurable and all that, but it had never been anything but fun. Tanzil brought a level of intensity and care that laid him bare, and Logan found himself falling for the Warden with a soft and somewhat tattered heart.

Reaching down, Logan stroked his cock. Tanzil leaned forward, balancing his weight on his arms. His lips sought Logan's, and as his cock thrust into Logan's ass, his tongue plundered Logan's sweet mouth.

Logan kept one hand on his cock, and the other explored Tanzil's skin. Insistent caresses turned to frantic scratches as passion exploded between them. Everything became frenzied. Logan locked his gaze with Tanzil's, and he noted how the cords on his alpha's neck stood out as he grunted with the effort it took to stave off the inevitable. He realized Tanzil was just as swept away by passion as he was, and he took comfort in how he affected his lover.

"Warden." He used Tanzil's title at a lover's caress, and the pace of his hand on his cock increased.

All of a sudden, Tanzil hooked an arm under Logan's leg, hiking it up to give him better access. He thrust hard twice, and then he cried out his climax.

Logan's orgasm loomed close.

Tanzil watched as he pulled his softening cock from Logan's body, the predatory light in his gaze betraying his intent. "That's it, omega. Come for me." Leaning down, he tongued Logan's sac, taking a ball into his mouth and sucking hard.

The unexpected pain made him cry out, and his orgasm detonated. Waves of pleasure washed through Logan, and before they were gone, Tanzil lapped up Logan's semen from his stomach and from the sensitive tip of his cock.

He held Logan in his arms as the tremors of their pleasure settled.

"I figure you've got about a week or so before the roads open." Tanzil pressed a kiss to Logan's forehead.

A smile curved Logan's mouth. He had a week of bliss ahead of him. He flicked his tongue across Tanzil's dusky nipple.

Tanzil rolled Logan onto his back and pinned his hands beside his head. "How was your time at the river?"

"Productive. Sort of." He thought about the peace he'd found. "I felt the Wards, just like you said I would. It was amazing. I've never felt like I belonged anywhere, and now I have a sense of my place as a shifter."

"That's wonderful." Surprise widened Tanzil's eyes. "Not many bears ever understand that."

Logan felt a sense of accomplishment, but that didn't bring answers. "I just don't know what I'm supposed to do with that."

"You'll find your way, omega. I have faith in you." Tanzil leaned down and captured Logan's lips for another searing kiss.

Chapter 8—Logan

A car door closed outside. Logan lifted his head from where it rested on Tanzil's chest. "Are you expecting company?"

In the two weeks since he'd been there, he'd seen nobody except Tanzil. They'd fallen into a routine that included having breakfast and dinner together, most of which Logan cooked. It turned out Tanzil could make two dishes—soup and chili.

Logan spent time at the river every day, but he returned in time to tend to the pumpkins in Tanzil's garden. His ministrations had fended off mildew, and three pumpkins were thriving because he turned them every day. Then he'd make dinner and wish he had better clothes to wear for when Tanzil got home. He needed shirts to bring out the blue in his eyes and pants that better showed off the shape of his ass.

This morning, his lover had lingered after breakfast, and the two of them had ended up back in bed.

Tanzil went to the bedroom window overlooking the front of the house. He moved aside the translucent curtain and peered out. "Get dressed."

Logan slid his legs into his jeans, something Tanzil had in his backpack from when he'd tracked him. It was nice to wear a pair of pants that fit him, though he'd spent a lot of time naked—either in bear form or because he couldn't seem to get enough of Tanzil.

Tanzil donned his brown uniform, and Logan's heart sank. It looked like his lover was going to work after all. Given the visitor, he hoped nothing serious had happened. He followed Tanzil down the stairs as their visitor knocked. "Who's here?"

Pressing his lips together, Tanzil sighed. "Your ride."

He twisted the doorknob to open the door, and Logan slammed his hand against the flat of the wood to keep it shut. "My ride? You knew about this, and you didn't tell me?"

Tanzil met Logan's gaze and exhaled. "I didn't know they were coming, but I'm not surprised they're here. Are you going to move so I can open the door?"

Feeling betrayed, though he had no idea why, he scooted out of the way.

Tanzil opened the door to reveal Logan's fathers, Marlin and Arlen. A smile split Marlin's stoic face, and tears streamed down Arlen's face.

Now Logan felt like an ass. He'd talked to his fathers a few times since he'd been with Tanzil, but he'd been too wrapped up in his lover to really think about the people he'd left behind who were worried about him.

The screen door flung open, and his fathers scooped him up in a tight hug. He melted into that paternal embrace, holding Marlin's hand tight while he patted Arlen's shoulder.

"I'm okay." He heard himself murmur assurances and quiet platitudes to ease their minds. "Really. I'm fine."

When his fathers finally released him a good while later, Cord Bearsmith shook his hand briefly before pulling him in for a hug. "You're looking well."

"I feel fine." Free of the tangle of arms, Logan glanced around, searching for Tanzil. He found him standing by the stairs, leaning against the banister. He motioned him forward. "Dad, Father, I'd like you to meet Tanzil Jareth."

Tanzil offered a hand, but he found himself swallowed in a mass of hugs.

"You saved my baby's life," Arlen sobbed. "I can never thank you enough for that."

Marlin echoed the sentiment in a weak voice.

Logan glanced at Sheriff Bearsmith while Tanzil endured affection. "Thanks for coming."

The sheriff looked from him to Tanzil and back. "No problem. Chase wanted to come, but he was afraid to leave the baby."

While he'd been gone, his best friend had welcomed a baby boy into the world. "I understand. I'll see him when I get back."

Arlen slapped his cheek lightly. "All this fresh air and sunshine has done wonders for you, Logan. I've never seen you look so healthy and happy."

"Arlen, leave the boy alone. He's been through enough."

"Can I offer anyone something to drink?" Tanzil's offer rang hollow, and Logan peered at his alpha.

No, he wasn't his alpha any longer. As he watched, Tanzil abdicated that role.

"Sure." Sheriff Bearsmith took off his hat and set it on the table behind the sofa. "And lunch. And the bathroom."

Tanzil pointed the way to the downstairs bathroom. Arlen threw his arms around Logan's neck once more as Cord and Tanzil disappeared into the kitchen.

"Tell me," Arlen said. "I want to know everything that happened."

Logan shook his head. "I've been through it all with Warden. I mean, Tanzil. He's easy to talk to about stuff like that. I'm okay, Father. I promise."

Tanzil made sandwiches, and he barely looked at Logan during the meal. By the time everyone headed out to the sheriff's car, Logan felt like he'd been dismissed from Tanzil's life.

It was as if the last two weeks together hadn't happened.

A fist squeezed his chest.

Tanzil waited outside the car, speaking in low tones to Sheriff Bearsmith, a serious expression on both their faces. In the back seat, Logan stared, feasting for the last time on the visage of the man who'd save his life and stolen his heart.

The sheriff got in and started the engine.

"I'll be right back." Logan shot out of the car and ran to the house.

Tanzil stood on the porch, his shoulders square and his eyes soft with affection.

"You're not going to say anything?"

The alpha's gaze sidled away. "I hope you found what you were looking for."

The wish hit Logan like a slap across the face. "That's it? After everything we shared, that's all?"

Tanzil inhaled sharply. "Logan, I don't know what else to say. I'm twelve years older than you. I'm in a different place in my life. You're starting out. Your future is still before you, waiting for you to decide on a path. Mine is set in stone. I'm a widower who's still mourning his husband. I wouldn't trade my time with you for anything except maybe to erase the terrible things that have happened to you. I'd give it all up to make it so that never happened." He trailed his fingertips over Logan's cheek. "You're a special man, and I wish you nothing but the best."

He didn't know what he expected. Tanzil had been honest with him the whole time. Logan closed his eyes against the stab of pain in his heart. He'd been naïve to think he had a chance with Tanzil. He turned his face away from Tanzil's caress. "You're full of shit, Warden. One day you'll realize you're not still mourning Namir. You're just afraid to love again. You're a coward who's afraid of actually living."

Rather than see the stricken expression he knew was on Tanzil's face, he returned to the car. He got inside and stared straight ahead.

Marlin occupied the seat next to him. He reached over and threaded his fingers through Logan's. Thankfully he didn't say a word about what he'd seen.

74

As they neared Bear's Cove, Arlen started to press his agenda. "You should come home with us. I'm sure you don't want to be alone."

More than anything, he wanted to be alone so he could wallow in his broken heart and try to come to terms with the hand he'd been dealt. But the moment he made it to Bear's Cove, he was deluged with visitors wanting to hug him and wish him well.

He missed Tanzil.

A week later, Logan's phone rang with an unfamiliar number. Normally he would let it go to voicemail, but this time he picked it up without thinking. That was maybe a by-product of the numbness he'd felt ever since he'd returned. His loved ones had chalked it up to post-traumatic stress, and they'd been supportive. Logan wouldn't talk about his ordeal with anyone, especially not the part that really tore at him—losing Tanzil.

Sure, they'd both gone into it with the idea it would be a temporary affair, a way to assuage the yearning of their inner bears. But somewhere along the line, Tanzil had come to mean a great deal more to Logan. He'd fallen in love with a man who spent his free time mourning another. Part of Logan understood. Tanzil had become part of him, and not a day passed that the ghost of his memory didn't invade his thoughts and leave him aching from the loss.

But another part of Logan resented Tanzil's stubborn insistence on perpetual mourning. Nobody who'd ever loved him would want him to live a shell of a life.

With a sigh, he said, "Hello?"

"Logan, this is Tanzil Jareth."

I know who you are, motherfucker. The thought came on the heels of resentment due to Tanzil's officious tone. *We were lovers. Why didn't I mean anything to you?*

Out loud, he strove for an equally neutral tone. "Hey."

"I'm calling to update you on the case. I'm having trouble communicating with my human counterpart due to the Wards. Protection is a double-edged sword sometimes."

Yeah. Logan knew that firsthand. He listened to Tanzil's update, and when his former lover asked him how he was doing, he kept it brief. "I'm fine. I'm back in Bear's Cove with my friends and family."

Every week, Tanzil called. Every week, they had the same conversation. While Tanzil spoke to him about warrants, charges, arrests, arraignments, and legal crap, Logan wrestled with anger and resentment. He mentally shouted at the man who'd kissed him as if he meant something, whose arms encircled him when he woke up sweating from a nightmare, and who'd nurtured his desire to find his path in life.

In the meantime, Logan had begun making baby clothes. The bear onesie had gone over well, and he had requests from all over Bear's Cove to make more. In addition, he was experimenting with other kinds of outfits for infants and toddlers. He selected soft, washable fabrics, and he found he had a knack for making clothes. Who would have guessed?

Arlen gifted him with a brand new sewing machine, and Logan happily spent hours cutting and sewing. He'd made his first outfit before he'd set out to find himself, and now he realized he'd stumbled upon a fulfilling line of work by chance before he'd even packed a bag.

Logan loved sewing. He set up a website featuring unique and limited-edition items, and he found himself busy filling orders for handmade infant and toddler clothes. If he kept going at this rate, he was going to have to hire people to help with the production process. Right now, he barely had time to himself, which was a good thing. He needed to keep busy.

One day, a few months later, Chase happened to be over with baby Ezra during one of Tanzil's utilitarian-toned update calls. When Logan ended the call, Chase gazed at him expectantly. "Are you going to tell him you're pregnant?"

Logan caressed the swell of his stomach. It had sprung up suddenly one morning when his jeans wouldn't fasten. His fathers were happy, though they'd have preferred for Logan to wait until he was married and settled down.

He cut a length of material. "Nope."

"Don't you think you owe it to him?"

"I don't owe him a thing." He motioned Chase closer. Mostly he needed Ezra. The baby served as a mannequin and model for his design process.

Chase brought Ezra, holding his arm still so Logan could measure it. "That fabric is perfect. Dak is going to love this."

He was making a miniature deputy uniform for Ezra.

Grinning at the little brown-haired baby smiling at him, he said, "So is Ezra. It's going to be comfortable, buddy. I promise."

"Seriously, Logan. I think Tanzil has a right to know."

"Agree to disagree."

"You're still angry with him, but it's not about you and him anymore. In a couple months, you're going to have a baby, and he or she deserves a chance to know both parents."

76

"Chase, I love you, but this is none of your business. My circumstances are different from yours. My baby daddy made it clear he doesn't want me. I gave him a chance, and he didn't take it."

With a sigh, Chase gave up. Logan didn't make the mistake of thinking Chase wouldn't keep harping on the issue, but at least he'd have peace—for now.

Chapter 9—Tanzil

"You could go see him, you know." Brock Bearsmith, Namir's cousin and Cord's husband, set a mug of coffee on the table.

Brock and Namir had much in common. They were both fine-boned with a slim build. Both had light brown hair, hazel eyes, and skin that would rather burn than tan. The four of them—Cord included—had once been close, but after Namir passed away and Tanzil had isolated himself, they'd drifted apart.

Tanzil hadn't come to Bear's Cove to see Brock. He'd come to see Cord, but Brock had waylaid him at the door to the station. Tanzil sipped the coffee. It had too much sugar and not enough cream, but he wasn't about to complain. "I'm here to see Cord."

Convincing the prosecutor outside the Wards to press charges had proven difficult. They kept forgetting he existed, and so they forgot about the case as well. It had taken six months to close the case, and Tanzil had found it necessary to master some offensive bear mysticism in addition to the defensive mysticism he'd learned to become a Warden.

Cord, of course, had been instrumental in helping him navigate the law-enforcement end of the issue. He'd called Tanzil to Bear's Cove to take care of the last of the paperwork. Tanzil thought his part had ended over a month ago, but as a conservation officer, he'd never been involved with a major crime like this before.

"So, they finally got a plea from those evil McConnells?" Brock stirred his coffee. "It's about time."

Tanzil shifted. "Is Cord here?"

"No. He's out." Brock set a hand on Tanzil's wrist. "Let's talk about you and me and Namir."

Namir. There was a name that crossed his mind less often, while Logan's weighed on it heavily. Though he was gone and Tanzil hadn't seen him in half a year, Logan was never far from his thoughts. Who the hell was he kidding? Logan occupied the vast majority of his thoughts and all of his fantasies.

A dull pang echoed through his core, half for Namir and half for Logan. "Namir's gone."

"I know that." Brock squeezed his wrist. "I was wondering if you'd realized it yet."

Tanzil got to his feet and paced around the table, coming to a stop in front of a window. "It's pretty fucking hard not to."

Brock's birdlike hands perched on his shoulders. "Look, Namir was a great guy. We all loved him. But he'd be the first to tell you that it's okay to move on."

A year ago he would have turned on Brock with a scathing verbal attack, lecturing him about loyalty and love. But now he understood what Brock had been trying to tell him for years. He patted one of the hands on his shoulders. "I know that now."

"Have you called Logan at all?"

"I call him every week to update him on the case." And every week, Logan listened and thanked him for his dedication to his job. They exchange exceedingly polite pleasantries, and then they ended the call. He couldn't quite get up the courage to ask Logan if he'd found his path in life, but he hoped for the best.

"Have you ever asked him how he's doing?"

Tanzil's stomach dropped, and he whirled to face Brock. "He always says he's fine. Why? What's wrong?"

Sadness reflected in Brock's hazel eyes, mixing with something that set off alarm bells in Tanzil's mind.

Without waiting for an answer, he grabbed his jacket and headed out of the station. He knew exactly where Logan lived because he'd finally installed an internet connection in his house, and he'd looked it up.

He navigated the wet streets. The air had warmed for spring, and piles of snow were in the midst of melting. Logan's small house wasn't far from the sheriff's post. He made it there in under ten minutes.

Two men stood on the walk in front of the house, and one of them was Logan. Tanzil would recognize the contours of his face and the way he stood anywhere. He held a baby in his arms while the other man lifted a second infant from the stroller. Though he hadn't seen a picture of Chase before, Logan had described his friend in detail, enough for Tanzil to identify him.

They'd paused when his car came to a stop along the curb in front of the house. Logan handed the child he was holding to Chase. His lips moved, and then Chase took both infants into the house.

Logan shuffled his feet nervously as Tanzil approached. His hair had grown back, and now it was long enough for Logan to brush his bangs off his forehead. "I wasn't expecting you."

"I was in town, so I thought I'd stop by."

"Cord said they pled guilty to lesser charges, and sentencing is next week. He said I should prepare a statement." A baby's cry came from inside the house, and Logan looked toward the sound. "Is that what you came to tell me?"

Was it? Brock hadn't said anything was wrong with Logan, but the melancholy in his expression had fairly shrieked. And Logan—he'd left Tanzil with a glow to his skin and a sparkle in his eyes, and now he looked tired and too thin. "Logan, is everything okay?"

"Yeah. Fine. Peachy. Couldn't be better."

Too many assurances rang false, as did the evidence in front of his face. Tanzil came closer, forcing Logan to tilt his head. It was an alpha move, but he couldn't keep from asserting a small bit of dominance. "Have you found your path?"

With a small shake of his head and a huge roll of his eyes, Logan stepped back. "I found my path. You're standing on it."

Like an idiot, Tanzil looked down at the walkway. "That's not what I meant."

Logan retreated another step. "Look, thanks for going the extra mile. I appreciate all you've done to seek justice for what happened to me. I'm happy to put it all behind me." He turned and went up the two steps to the cement porch.

Tanzil couldn't seem to let him go. "You aren't happy."

With his back to Tanzil, Logan froze. "Neither are you. But then again, I'm not sure you'd know what to do if happiness fell into your lap."

A wry bark of laughter fell from his lips and clattered to the ground in all its pathetic glory. Happiness had fallen into his lap—and it had taken up residence in his home for a too-brief moment in time. "I pushed it away. I told myself it wasn't for me, that I didn't deserve it."

Logan's hand clutched the knob on the door.

Tanzil panicked. For the first time in forever, he spoke without thinking, and it came directly from the heart. "I miss you. Not a day goes by that I don't think about you."

"You're obsessed with my case because you couldn't save your husband. I'm your chance at penance." Anguish twisted the omega's words, rendering them not more than a whisper.

Climbing the steps, he stopped inches from Logan's back. Tension radiated from the lines in his body, and he knew Logan was seconds from breaking. "I knew the road was open, and I put off telling you because I didn't want you to go. But I didn't know how to ask you to stay." He swayed closer, drinking in Logan's scent. "I fell in love with you, but I didn't think I deserved to have someone as wonderful as you in my life. I didn't think I deserved happiness."

Logan stood as still as a statue. "What's changed?"

"Everything. I stopped worshipping Namir's memory. I stopped beating myself up. I've worked to become the man you thought I was."

The wails of a baby started up again. Logan turned, his body moving in increments. That sky blue gaze held him captive. "I have to get inside."

Tanzil's hand shot out, wrapping around Logan's arm. "Give me a chance. That's all I'm asking for."

Logan jerked a thumb in the direction of the door. "How about I give you a chance to meet your daughter? She's the one in there with the impressive set of lungs who wants her diaper changed."

Stunned, Tanzil lost his grip on Logan's arm.

Logan went inside, and the crying eased.

The door opened, and the other man came out carrying a car seat with a quiet baby inside. He grinned and stuck out a hand. "You're Tanzil. I'm Chase. Dak Freeman is my husband. You've talked on the radio quite a bit. It's great to finally meet you."

Dak had been one of the few willing to feed him tidbits of information about Logan, but it looked like he'd left out a huge and important piece. Numbly, he shook Chase's hand.

"You should go in," Chase said. "Alara is completely adorable, except for when she's dirty or hungry. Then she turns into a total diva, just like Logan."

Tanzil moved out of the way to let Chase pass, and then he went inside. The house was small and dark by virtue of the tiny windows. He followed the hall light to a room in the rear of the house.

Logan stood next to a table, zipping the front of a pink jogging outfit as he talked to the tiny baby waving her arms.

Tanzil came closer. He peered at the baby on the changing table. She had honeyed skin and chocolate eyes, and she sported a shock of black hair on her head. Her arms flailed wildly when she saw him.

"Looks like someone is excited." Logan lifted her in his arms, cradling her to his chest. "Tanzil, this is Alara. Alara, meet your daddy."

He couldn't breathe. A weight pressed on his chest. Wetness blurred his vision, and it took him several moments to identify what was happening.

Happiness. This was happiness.

He slid his arms around Logan, hugging the man he loved and their daughter to him. "Thank you for this, my omega."

After too short of a time, Alara protested this arrangement with a coughing noise.

"Is she sick?"

"No. She's hungry. That's her way of asking for food. If I don't feed her fast enough, then she cries." Logan handed Alara over. "Make funny faces at her while I warm up a bottle."

He left, and Tanzil found himself alone with a little girl who looked remarkably like him. His whole life, he'd wanted to be a father. He'd dreamed of filling his house with lots of kids, of having a home bursting to the seams with the laughter of children. And now his dream had come true.

Hadn't it? Logan hadn't exactly responded to his confession of stupidity and declaration of love.

He tried to make faces, but all he could do was smile. Just by existing, this little girl had captured his heart and wrapped him around her tiny finger. He fed Alara her bottle until she fell asleep in his arms. Logan took her from him and set her in a crib. Then he took Tanzil by the hand and led him from the room, not stopping until they were in the kitchen.

"Want some tea? I stopped drinking coffee when I was pregnant."

Logan had kept his pregnancy from Tanzil. All those calls, and he hadn't once indicated that he was having a baby. And then he'd given birth—alone, as he'd been throughout his pregnancy—and he still hadn't said a word to Tanzil.

This distressed Tanzil, but he didn't hold it against Logan. This was another thing he'd missed out on due to his obstinate insistence that his life could never improve, that he couldn't achieve his dreams—that there was no such thing as a second chance.

And he'd been so very wrong.

He backed Logan up until he was trapped between his body and the counter. "You never answered me."

Logan's tongue darted out to lick his lower lip. "I don't remember the question."

"I told you that I love you, and I was stupid for letting you walk out of my life."

Logan's gaze dropped. "I'm still twelve years younger than you. That's never going to change."

"I'll have to learn to live with that." Tanzil cracked a brief smile. "My husband is young and hot. Such a hardship."

"I, um, I found my path in life."

"Yeah? Whatever it is, I'll support it."

"It turns out I'm really good at designing cute baby clothes. Did you notice Alara's outfit?"

Tanzil had not noticed anything other than it was a soft pink. "I was too busy being blown away by the fact that I'm a father."

Logan laughed, and the simple joy of it washed through Tanzil's consciousness, a balm for so much pain. His hand teased a line up Tanzil's chest. "I have a website. I'm doing pretty good business."

82

"Fuck, Logan. I'm on board—you can take over the whole basement for your business—but you're killing me. Is there a chance for us?"

All pretense fell away from Logan's face, and his pure gaze held Tanzil's. "Yes. I love you, Warden—heart and soul."

Tanzil leaned down and brushed his lips against Logan's. "Marry me."

Logan's arms twined around his alpha's neck. "Anything you want, Warden."

"I want you." Tanzil claimed his omega with a searing kiss.

About A. J. Stone

A.J. Stone loves rainbows and bears. Visit https://michelezurloauthor.com/a-j-stone/ for the latest information or follow on Facebook at https://www.facebook.com/AJStoneBearsCove/ to keep up with the newest releases, and feel free to request stories for your favorite Bear's Cove characters.

Reviews let A.J. know you want more!

Bear's Cove Series (MM/MPreg) by A. J. Stone

Dak's Omega
Tanzil's Second Chance
Perfect Blend: Kofi's Omega

Draco International Series (MM/MPreg) by A. J. Stone

Amaricio's Omega Shifter
Koren's Omega Neighbor
Zeke's Reluctant Omega

MM Romance by Nicoline Tiernan

Nexus #1: Tristan's Lover by Nicoline Tiernan
Nexus #2: The Man of His Dreams by Nicoline Tiernan

Sneak Peek at Perfect Blend: Kofi's Omega

If marrying the wrong man made for a regrettable start to adult life, what kind of mistake was it for a man to move to the same town his ex had moved to?

And was it worse if that man wanted to open up a business in that town, sort of start over in the same place his ex had started over?

Hoyt thought about that as he considered the piece of real estate surrounding him. He chewed his bottom lip as he thought.

The idea to open a coffee shop wasn't a bad idea. Bear's Cove had three, but they could use one closer to the waterfront. He could sell sandwiches and pastries or whatever struck his fancy. This lease space had room on the east side for patio dining, where bear shifters could dare seagulls to mess with them while they ate.

Coffee shops were natural meeting places. They brought people together for all types of events, from friends meeting for a quick cup to business people meeting to discuss their next big deal to two bears meeting for the first time — organically, not the arranged kind of meeting.

While he could have refused the match all those years ago, he had gone through with it from a sense of obligation to his family and his community. So had his ex. Hoyt wanted to make it possible for bears to meet compatible mates and have fun while doing it.

That's why the working title for his new business was Grind-N-Growl.

Bear's Cove was a perfect city, perched on the edge of the sea but still nestled away on hills and surrounded by forests. Hoyt had never considered moving there until he'd visited on that fateful day six months ago when nobody in his ex-husband's family could find his ex to tell him that his fathers had passed away.

Hoyt couldn't turn down that call. He wasn't heartless. Divorce didn't mean he'd stopped caring for Dak, only that he'd finally admitted that they weren't in love. Their joining had lacked passion and joy. Sometimes there had been enthusiasm, but that was mostly when Hoyt closed his eyes and pretended he was fucking someone else. Likely Dak had done the same thing.

Hoyt wanted passion and joy. Dak, his ex-husband, had found those things with his new husband, Chase. The only bit of jealousy or resentment Hoyt harbored was that he'd been unable to also find those things. It wasn't fair. He'd left Dak so they could both find happiness. He'd gone off to look for love, and Dak had moved to Bear's Cove to be a deputy. Dak hadn't even been looking for the love that had fallen into his lap. Lucky bastard.

Hoyt had searched through most of the protected lands where bear shifters roamed, but nowhere he visited seemed quite right. The moment he'd stepped foot into Bear's Cove, he felt like he'd found the place where he belonged.

Chase was on board with Hoyt's business plan, especially once Hoyt mentioned opening a coffee shop. Hoyt liked Chase. They were both omegas, and perhaps under other circumstances, the two would have forged a close friendship. What they had now was polite and a little awkward. Hoyt wished it wasn't. Chase had given birth to Ezra, the cutest baby in the world, a few months ago, and Hoyt wanted to spoil the infant in a way only a favored uncle could. Except he wasn't an uncle.

Ulysses, the real estate agent with an ambitious name, grinned. "It's already set up with a commercial kitchen. You won't have to make many changes."

With a sigh, he peered out the windows fronting the store. "Get me the contract on this one so I can read it." Not being an expert on real estate or lease contracts, he wanted to have someone he trusted look them over before he made a commitment. Even if he couldn't get anyone to do him the favor of reading the contracts and giving their opinion, at the very least, he wanted to look everything over on his own.

"I'll send it to your email address." Ulysses tapped away on his phone. "If you have any question, feel free to ask me. That's what you're paying me for."

While he trusted Ulysses, there was someone Hoyt trusted more. After viewing several more potential sites, Hoyt retired to his hotel room on the outskirts of town. He showered and dressed in comfortable pajamas bottoms, then he sat on the bed and stared at his phone.

An eternity passed, and then he pressed the button to make the call. Kofi Freeman was his ex-brother-in-law and the man he'd originally thought he was slated to marry. The pair hadn't spoken since Hoyt attended the funeral for the Freemans' fathers half a year ago.

Six years older than either Hoyt or Dak, Kofi had rarely been around. Almost as soon as Hoyt and Dak's engagement had been announced, Kofi had bowed to wanderlust. He'd stayed in the area long enough to attend the engagement party, and he'd returned for the wedding. Other than that, he spent the vast majority of his time globetrotting, returning to Forrest Hills only twice each year.

Hoyt knew that in his travels, Kofi had experienced just about every job known to man, including working a stint as a leasing agent for a prominent resort company. Of course, he tried to keep his real job — a novelist who wrote shifter romances — a secret, but they all knew of his literary accomplishments. Hoyt had read them all many times. Kofi was the smartest shifter Hoyt had ever met, and there was nobody whose opinion Hoyt trusted more.

"Hello?" The voice on the other end of the line was low and silky.

Hoyt closed his eyes, picturing Kofi reclining in a lounger on a beach somewhere exotic, watching the sunset. In his imagination, Kofi wore loose shorts with a tropical pattern. His bare chest glistened in the setting sun, and those full lips closed over the long neck of a bottle of summer lager.

Hoyt's imagination was running away to a wonderful and forbidden place. He forced it to stop. "Kofi, this is Hoyt."

"I know." A smooth chuckle encouraged him to continue. "How are you?"

"I'm, um, I'm okay, I guess." Yep, now was an excellent time for Hoyt to turn into a stammering idiot. "How are you?"

"I'm well."

The other end went silent, reminding Hoyt that he was the one who'd called. "Look, I'm sorry to bother you, but I, um, I didn't know who else to call."

The wind and bird calls in the background went away. "What's wrong?"

Hoyt realized his hemming and hawing had triggered Kofi's worry buttons, and he scrambled to fix the situation. "Nothing's wrong. I was looking at real estate today because I'm thinking I want to open a coffee shop. You know, the kind that maybe serves pastries or breakfast wraps or whatever I feel like making? I was thinking I'd keep it loose, like when customers come in, it'll be a surprise what's on the menu."

"Hoyt, take a breath." The worry in Kofi's tone was gone, replaced with a bit of humor.

Hoyt blushed, heat rising to suffuse his cheeks. He rambled. Words were his curse. When he was nervous or excited, they poured out of him at a million miles an hour. It had annoyed the hell out of Dak, and whenever Kofi had visited, Hoyt had struggled to slap a gag on his inner monologue that was often an outer one as well.

"Sorry. I shouldn't have called. I'm bothering you."

"You're not bothering me. I just don't want you passing out when there's no one around to catch you."

The heat in his cheeks flamed hotter. He'd love to protest that he wasn't that bad, but he regularly talked so much that he made himself dizzy. "I'm laying back on a bed, so if that should happen, I'll be fine."

A groan came from the other end.

"Are you okay? Did I interrupt something? I can call back later, or never, if this is just too weird." The rules for contacting the brother of one's ex-husband were murky, at best. And if one had spent the past decade lusting after that man, then there were additional complications.

"You're fine. I'm hanging out alone tonight, and I had absolutely no plans. You're not interrupting anything."

"Oh." Hoyt had expected to have to cram his request into the space between breaths and then work a lot of begging in alongside it. "I don't know which one to lease."

"Which what?"

"Space. I spent the day looking at spaces to lease for my coffee shop, Grind-N-Growl."

"Grind-N-Growl?"

"Yes, you know, for coffee and bears?"

Kofi made a thoughtful noise. "Hoyt, don't take this the wrong way, but that names kind of sounds like a bar or dance club — a place people might go to hook up."

Two minutes ago, the name had a clever ring inside Hoyt's head. Now it wasn't so great. He wanted people to find their perfect mate, not hook up for a quick one-night stand. "Like, I'll hook them up with coffee?"

"Coffee is not the first thing that comes to mind."